BROWN DWARF

ALSO BY K.D. MILLER

Holy Writ (The Porcupine's Quill, 2001)

Give Me Your Answer (The Porcupine's Quill, 1999)

A Litany in Time of Plague (The Porcupine's Quill, 1994)

POETRY CHAPBOOKS:

End Papers (Red Claw Press, 2010)

Psalms of a Boomer Consumer (Red Claw Press, 2009)

Counting the Ways (Red Claw Press, 2009)

Poeggs (Red Claw Press, 2009)

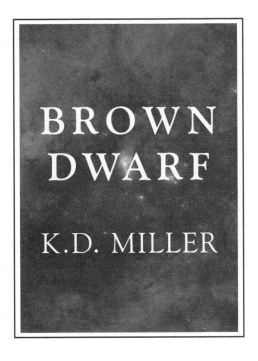

BROWN DWARF

K.D. MILLER

BIBLIOASIS

FIRST EDITION

Library and Archives Canada Cataloguing in Publication

Miller, K. D. (Kathleen Daisy), 1951-
     Brown dwarf / K.D. Miller.

ISBN 978-1-89723-88-3

     I. Title.

PS8576.I5392B76 2010   C813'.54   C2010-900983-5

Canada Council **Conseil des Arts**
for the Arts **du Canada**

Canadian   Patrimoine
Heritage   canadien

ONTARIO ARTS COUNCIL
CONSEIL DES ARTS DE L'ONTARIO

Biblioasis acknowledges the ongoing financial support of the Government of Canada through The Canada Council for the Arts, Canadian Heritage, the Book Publishing Industry Development Program (BPIDP); and the Government of Ontario through the Ontario Arts Council.

PRINTED AND BOUND IN CANADA

Dedicated to Mike Barnes
and Heather Simcoe

ACKNOWLEDGEMENTS

While writing this book, I was supported and encouraged in many ways by many people. I am grateful to the following publishers and publications for recommending different versions of *Brown Dwarf* for Ontario Arts Council Writers' Reserve grants: Biblioasis; Descant; The New Quarterly; The Porcupine's Quill; Thomas Allen Publishers.

I wish to thank the following individuals for their close reading and wise commentary: Kim Aubrey; Mike Barnes; Elaine Batcher; Mary Borsky; Melinda Burns; Sherry Coman; Deborah Kipp; Andrew Macrae.

I am indebted to Dan Wells, a publisher who reads with an editor's eye, for seeing the potential of *Brown Dwarf* to stand alone. And as always, I owe a warm thank-you to John Metcalf, editor and friend, for keeping the faith and welcoming the prodigal home.

BROWN DWARF

Brenda

B renda stares down at her saddle shoes. Navy and white, the navy parts like twin masks. When she wiggles her toes the white leather dimples like skin.

Jori is waiting for her. The way she always does. With her hands in her pockets and her head tilted back. Staring lazy-eyed out over the city. Just as if she doesn't mind that Brenda's holding them up. Again.

The white parts of Brenda's saddle shoes were clean this morning. Now there are black scuff marks on them, and a smudge of dirt on one of her socks. She wishes she had thin, plain socks like Jori's. Popcorn-stitch makes her ankles look thicker than they already are. But there's more to popcorn-stitch, her mother says. They're better value.

Jori is still waiting. She walked the ledge in seconds, just as if it was nice and flat and wide like the rest of the path. She didn't inch along the way Brenda's going to soon, holding her breath, grabbing at weeds that might pull out, clinging to corners of rock that might loosen and come away in her hand.

The first time Brenda made it across, Jori said, *I'm proud of you, Brenda Bray.* Brenda couldn't look at her. Didn't dare open her mouth in case she'd scream or cry. She had never hated any-one, not even Annie Bray, as much as she hated Jori Clement at that moment. And every time since then, she stands for long minutes thinking, *I can't I can't I can't.* Then all at once it's as if her feet think, *Yes you can.* And she hates Jori all over again.

Now the waistband of her skirt is starting to bind. She was going to wear slacks, but her mother made her change out of them because they'd gotten too tight for her to wear outside the house where all the world could see her. They looked indecent, Annie Bray said. (Sometimes Brenda lets herself think *Annie Bray* instead of *my mother.* She's starting to do it more and more, especially when her mother says things like *indecent.*) All her other slacks were in the wash, so she had to put on a skirt. And that meant she had to put on her saddle shoes, because you can't wear running shoes with a skirt. Just like you can't go to church without a hat, or carry a white purse before the twenty-fourth of May.

She could tell Jori was surprised by the way she was dressed. Jori was in her usual Saturday outfit – blue jeans and a white T-shirt with a tan windbreaker over it and boys' running shoes – the black and white kind with the red rubber circle at the ankle. (*I get my clothes in the boys' department. Daddy hates it, but Mummy tells him it's just a phase.*) Brenda kept expecting her to say some-thing – *What the hell are you doing in a skirt?* Or, *Jesus, Brenda Bray, we're not going to a tea party.* But she didn't. She hasn't said any of the other things Brenda keeps expecting her to say, either. *How much do you weigh? What size do you take?*

Brenda's feet still won't move. Maybe there's a safety rule against walking a ledge in saddle shoes. What if she fell and broke her neck? Or worse, what if she fell and didn't die, but got hurt so badly that her mother had to push her around in a wheelchair? *If you'd done what I told you. If you'd stayed away from that Jori or whatever she calls herself.* Day after day, for the rest of their lives.

It's not really very steep here. If she did fall, she'd probably just scrape her knees and elbows. But she might rip her skirt, too, her perfectly good skirt that still has lots of wear in it and that cost good money. Annie Bray would demand to know how she did it, and would keep on at her until it all came out. Who she was with. What she was doing. Where. The where would be the worst part. No. Maybe the what. Except the who would be pretty bad too. There is absolutely nothing good about what they are doing right now. Not a single thing. And Jori is still waiting.

That waistband is almost cutting her in half. Brenda hopes it hasn't rolled itself into a rope, because then the label might show at the back and Jori might see *For the Pleasingly Plump Child* stitched in pink thread.

"I'm sorry I'm taking so long," she calls. It's what she always says when they get stuck at the ledge.

Jori shrugs. "Take as long as you want." That's what she always answers. As if the two of them had just stopped for a minute to look at the view.

The city doesn't look quite real to Brenda today. The bright October sun makes the shadows sharp. The streets could have been drawn with a ruler, they run in such straight lines down to the bay, and the tiny houses look perfect from this high up. No missing shingles or broken bricks or sagging porches. The trees look like somebody painted them green then shook drops of orange and yellow over them. Even the smoke from the steel plants is like something in a painting, shooting straight up into the pure blue sky. Brenda imagines the tiny people who live down there leading perfect little lives with no *Pleasingly Plump* labels and no Hurricane Annies and no ledges to cross and no Jori Clements waiting for them.

Jori is still waiting, with that cool smile of hers smoothing her mouth. *Why doesn't she just leave me here?* Brenda thinks. *What does she want with me, anyway? Wouldn't she be better off without me?*

She looks up into the sky. This would be the perfect time for her father to come rattling down out of the clouds in his bus. He would lift his Hamilton Street Railway cap to her and say, *Hop aboard, Miss Bray!* Then together they would drive up, up and away, for ever and ever amen.

She's had that daydream for as long as she can remember. But ever since she's known Jori, she's been asking herself stupid questions, almost as if she wants to spoil it. *How would your father recognize you, since he only ever saw you as a baby? Would he be disappointed at the way you turned out? Would you still be Pleasingly Plump in heaven?* Twelve is too old for daydreams. She can just hear Annie Bray – *A big girl like you.*

Her feet still won't take the first step onto the ledge. "I'm coming," she calls. "Soon."

Jori smiles. Says, "I know you are."

Rae

Two words. That's all I ever wrote in this diary you gave me. The handwriting is mine, but not mine. Sweetly rounded, and oh so careful. The very first words in my brand new book.

It's probably an antique now. 1962 stamped in gold on the spine. Brown nubbly leather binding. And the pages when I ruffle them still smelling like then.

I was in my hospital bed when I wrote those two words. The nurses were feeding me baby food. Every time I woke up, this teaspoon would be coming at me with a little mound of orange mush on it. Some hawk-eyed Nightingale watching to see that I swallowed. Escorting me to the bathroom to make sure I didn't stick my finger down my throat.

They all perked up after a week or so when I asked for a book to write in. And not just any book, either. Oh no. It had to be the one that my officially still-missing friend had given me. Ah, I could practically hear them thinking. Therapy.

So Annie Bray got it out of my locker at school and brought it to me. It was the first she knew about it, and she must have been dying to open it. Would have found nothing but blank pages if she had. When she handed it to me and found me a pen, she leaned forward to watch, all big-eyed and eager. "Go home," I told her. And she did.

Dear Jori is as far as I got. When I saw your name in my own handwriting, I started to cry and couldn't stop. That perked the nurses up even more. Ah. Catharsis. Well, they were a little premature. I never wrote in this book again. Until now.

I'm sitting in a Starbucks in Hamilton, Jori. Looking out on Concession Street. Our old beat. I promised myself I'd never set foot in this burg again, but here I am. I can almost see you sitting across from me. *What are you writing, Brenda Bray?* Then you'd reach and grab and see for yourself. Just the way you did – my God. Forty-six years ago.

Would you even recognize me? I'm thin and sharp and silver now, like an old knife. Maybe you'd pick me out of the lineup right away. I always had the feeling you were looking through me – through the fat, that is. Seeing something that just needed to surface, the way my cheekbones did. And somewhere in the back of my mind I've had the feeling you were watching me all these years, that you were present somehow. Whenever something big happened – the Beatles, Kennedy's assassination, the Berlin Wall coming down, the Twin Towers – I would imagine you taking it in with those cool green eyes of yours. Maybe that's why my gut reaction to the news that your body might have been found was disappointment.

You wouldn't have thought much of the header that caught my eye on page three of the *Toronto Star*: HUMAN REMAINS FOUND ON HAMILTON ESCARPMENT. No, not worthy of your scrapbook. Too sedate. Even though it did contain one of your favourite words. You used to just about lick your chops when you said it. *Remaaaaaains*. Make it sound all black and soupy and crawling with bugs.

I wish you really were here, sitting across from me. I wish I could say, "Jori, was that you?" All they could tell was that the bone was human, probably female, age estimated between twelve and fourteen. And that it had been there for at least twenty years, probably longer. A man was walking his dog along the path under the lip of the escarpment. The dog ducked into a crack in the cliff wall and came back with what looked like a stick in its mouth. Except the man was a chiropractor, and he knew a tibia when he saw one. So your name was in the paper again, Jori, and your cold case began to warm up.

For weeks I hunched over the *Star* every morning, scanning for the words, *last seen by childhood friend Brenda Bray*. I even started getting the *Spectator*. I kept expecting the phone to ring. Or maybe two of Hamilton's finest to show up at the door. "Rae Brand? Formerly Brenda Bray? May we come in? We have some questions regarding a statement you made to the police in 1962."

Not that I was worried. I had, technically, nothing to worry about. And if I could handle being questioned by the police at age twelve, I could sure as hell deal with it now. Besides, I figured, it might give the books a boost. . . . *Last seen by Brenda Bray, now Rae Brand, author of the popular Elsinor Grey series . . .* Never hurts for a mystery writer to have a real mystery in her past.

But it didn't happen. The tests on the tibia were inconclusive. You went back to being *missing, last seen in 1962*. Officially, that is. But as far as I was concerned, Jori, you were back. And so, thanks to you, was Brenda. In spite of everything I'd done, all those years ago, to get rid of her.

As soon as I got home from the hospital, I stripped my room. Took Brenda's school projects down from the walls. Put all her merit diplomas and Pleasingly Plump clothes into cardboard boxes. I'd have thrown it all away, but Annie Bray kept following me around, bleating. Next I went into training to be a teenager.

15

Subscribed to *Seventeen* magazine and *Ingenue*. Discovered flavoured lipstick and the colour hot pink. Hung my dresser mirror with scarves and beads. Grew out that Betty Windsor home perm. And once a week, I cleaned my room to within an inch of its life. Took everything off my dresser and shelves and dusted all the surfaces. Tidied my already tidy drawers. Washed the tiles of my floor with ammonia. When I was finished, the place smelled like the hospital I'd just left.

But there was still my name. I couldn't change it legally. Not yet. But I intended to be ready, the second I turned twenty-one. I couldn't find a perfect anagram that worked, so I threw away the Y and one of the B's to create Rae Brand. Rae Brand. I liked it. I liked being monosyllabic. I had always hated the teetering, rocking-chair sound of Bren-duh.

The only souvenir of my old life that I kept was this diary. Something about the thought of throwing it away spooked me. So I hung onto it all through high school. Took it with me to university. Packed and unpacked it every time I moved.

But I never wrote in it. Until now.

And look at how many pages I've filled. Well, it's an old trick. If you want to get your hand moving, choose a muse. Picture somebody in your mind and write to them.

I guess I was doing that instinctively when I wrote *Dear Jori* all those years ago. Not that it helped. Not at the time. My hand got stopped in its tracks. Maybe because it wasn't sure whose hand it was.

Brenda

The little train comes out of the papier mâché mountain, circles the little town, curves up and over the little bridge then disappears back inside the mountain. Round and round. The town has a train station, a white steepled church and a general store. A tiny lady in a long blue dress holds a little boy by the hand outside the church. A tiny man in a yellow shirt stands on the station platform, his hand raised to hail the train that never stops for him.

The model train set has been in the window of Boone's Hobbies on Concession Street for as long as Brenda can remember. And as long as she can remember, she has wished she could be the little man in the yellow shirt who stands forever on the platform, waiting for the train. It wouldn't matter that the train didn't stop, because there would always be the next time, and the next, and the next. Just as if time was standing still.

But she's not that little man. And time isn't standing still. Watching the train set can't even slow it down. Any more than taking the long way home from school can, on Hurricane Annie days.

There. Jori's signal. A slight turn of her head, then a slow, sly blink. She's decided that enough people have seen them. It's time to go inside the store and start their routine.

Brenda weaves up and down the aisles of Boone's Hobbies, following Jori. Pretending to be interested in coloured beads and felt squares and paint-by-number kits. It's never very long before Mr. Boone hears the two of them and pops up from behind a shelf, just as if he was part of the model train set.

"Hello, Mr. Boone!" Jori makes her voice smaller and younger-sounding than it is, and she sing-songs like a little kid. Brenda tries to do the same, but she's always half a syllable behind.

Mr. Boone reminds Brenda of a great big little boy with his round head and smooth chubby face. Inside his store he can be ten years old forever, collecting stamps and assembling model planes. Brenda wonders if that's why he never married. It would be too grown-up. Too normal. Annie Bray can name at least one not-normal thing about everybody on the mountain, and that's what she always says about Mr. Boone. That he never married.

"Know what?" Jori mutters once they've left his store after hearing his careful *Hello, young ladies*. "I think he's queer."

"Yeah. Maybe he is. A little." Brenda thinks she means peculiar. "But he's nice."

Jori gives her a look that means she's going to learn something once they're alone together on the escarpment face. Brenda always learns something from Jori. Sometimes she wishes she could forget it afterwards, like the time Jori went and got the *Marital Manual* out of her parents' bedroom.

"Won't your parents get mad?" Brenda whispered. She could hear Mrs. Clement setting out the sherry and lemonade in the living room. And that meant Professor Clement would be home any minute.

18

"Are you kidding? They showed me this when I was ten. Now look. See?" Jori pointed to a drawing of something that looked like a snake. Brenda knew it wasn't a snake, but she kept expecting a wormy, forked tongue to come out the hole. "I told you. It gets longer and thicker and harder and it sticks straight out. Now do you believe me?"

Their next stop after Boone's is Solly's Variety. Mr. Solly sells everything in his store – penny candy, Swiss Army Knives, baby dolls that drink and wet, bags of chips, bags of screws. Everything has a bloom of dust on it, as if it's been there forever, waiting for somebody to pay good money for it.

Brenda and Jori pull dripping bottles of pop out of a big red cooler that's filled with ice water and has the Coke sign on its side. "Hi, Mr. Solly," Jori says pointedly. That's Brenda's cue to echo, "Hi, Mr. Solly."

Mr. Solly's real name is Solomon Kandinsky, which makes him a foreigner. That's one not-normal thing about him that Annie Bray can name. The other is that he's a Jew. That's not really a bad thing, because Jesus was a Jew. But it's still not normal. Mr. Solly has a gap between his front teeth, but none between his eyebrows, and he's always the shiny tan colour of McIntosh toffee, even in the winter. Near the back of his store he has a refrigerated cabinet full of strange foods he calls deli. He makes smelly sandwiches for sale, thick with layers of cheeses and meats nobody's ever heard of. Annie Bray has told Brenda never to buy anything to eat from Mr. Solly, just to stick to bottled pop.

"Hello, Miss and Miss. You are fine this fine morning?"

There. He's seen them. He knows they were in his store. He'll back them up, too, if anyone tries to check their stories. "Oh yah," he'll say, sweating from smiling so hard. "I see them. Girl with red hair. And her friend the fa – the little bit chubby one. Every Saturday morning they come, to buy pop. Always the same kinds of pop. These kids, yah?"

Orange Crush for Brenda, Root Beer for Jori. All part of the trail they're leaving in peoples' memories. Same with their talk. "I don't know how you can go on drinking that stuff," Jori always says to Brenda. "It's positively juvenile." "Well," Brenda answers, trying to sound spunkier than she feels, "I don't know how you can drink that." To which Jori replies that Root Beer is an acquired taste.

Then on to Slaine's Notions and Dry Goods, where the door goes *ding*. "I'll do the buttons, you do the scarves," Jori mutters to Brenda at the last minute out on the sidewalk. She always picks two items at opposite ends of the store, because Mrs. Slaine is wall-eyed.

Inside, everything smells of lavender. There's a wall of pigeon holes at the back where balls of wool nestle like soft Easter eggs. At the front, there's a glass counter with ladies' gloves inside it, arranged palm to palm like praying hands.

"Just turn the button carousel," Mrs. Slaine pleads, her left eye rolling in Jori's direction. Her neck sways out like a vulture's from her widow's hump. "If you want to see the buttons at the back just turn it by the knob on the top. There is no need to – That is a silk scarf!" This to Brenda, whom she fixes with her right eye. "If you wish to see it, would you please allow me to unfold it for you?"

Brenda's embarrassed. Mrs. Slaine went to school with Annie Bray, and they see her every Sunday morning at Knox Presbyterian. She wishes she could tell her that they're not there to steal or to spill pop on her dry goods. They're just trying to be memorable.

"*Missus* Slaine," Jori says once they're back out on the sidewalk. "I bet. Can you imagine *Mister* Slaine? Can you imagine them doing it?"

20

"Doing what?"

The look again.

Brenda actually has a pretty good idea what, thanks to the *Marital Manual* and the thing that her mother always says about Mrs. Slaine. *Too much of a lady, that one. That's why no children. And why the mister is never at home.*

Last stop on Concession Street, Miss Hawkins at the Mountain Branch Public Library. Every Saturday, just as they're walking up to the library door, Jori changes. It only takes a second, and Brenda can never quite catch her doing it. But somewhere between the sidewalk and the book-lined hush of the library, she transforms into young Miss Marjorie Clement, who has just begun confirmation classes in preparation for her first Communion, which she will take the following Easter at Grace Church Anglican.

"My parents keep telling me not to do it unless I believe in it. They like to think they're so modern and open-minded. But they're friends with the Bishop, and I can tell they're all dewy-eyed about it already. So you know what I'm going to do when I have to kneel down in that stupid white dress and eat the Body and drink the Blood? I'm going to imagine I'm a captive pagan warrior queen who has to go through this ritual to save her people from being slaughtered wholesale by the Christians. Somebody kind of like Boadicea. What? Oh for Christ's sake, Brenda, don't you know anything? Boadicea was fantastic. She had razor-sharp blades on her chariot wheels, and she used to drive through a whole Roman legion and slice the soldiers' legs off at the knee."

So what? Brenda wants to say sometimes when Jori gets going. *You don't know everything.* She doesn't, either. Brenda just happens to know a few things herself. More than a few. Her mother sees to it that she does.

The night before an exam, Annie Bray drills her from the time the supper dishes are washed until bed. Drills her about Samuel de Champlain. The primary industries of Brazil. The Family Compact. The major land forms of Australia. Three hundred and fifty-seven point three divided by forty-nine point four.

"No!" she yells at a wrong answer. "No no no no no no no!" Then she imitates Brenda trying to list the characteristics of a marine west coast climate. "Now, be sure to start with the one you forgot last time," she says, all sweet and nasty. "And don't bother looking at that clock. You've still got an hour and a half."

But whenever Brenda brings home a report card, Annie Bray is her biggest fan. She goes over and over Brenda's marks while they eat supper. "Ninety-three in English! And you even got eighty in math! I could never do math at school. Anything to do with words or ideas, sure. I was great at that. But numbers? Never."

Brenda and Jori are inside the library, going up to Miss Hawkins' desk. Brenda dreads this part almost as much as she dreads crossing the ledge. It makes her wonder what she's doing with Jori Clement. Why she doesn't just tell her to go away and leave her alone and let her sit by herself again at recess. With her book.

"Um, Miss Hawkins?" Jori makes her eyes big and her voice tiny.

"Yes, dear?"

"Could you please tell me how many Mary Poppins books there are?"

An expression comes over the librarian's face that makes Brenda look down at her feet. Miss Hawkins has round blue eyes and a huge bosom. According to Annie Bray, she's starting to go a bit soft in the head the way women do when they never marry or have children.

"Oh, yes, dear!" Miss Hawkins sounds like she might cry. "I could tell you that. I'll just get this big book down from the top shelf. Oof! Now. It's P.L. Travers, isn't it? Travers. Travers. Ah. Here. My goodness. There seem to be quite a few. Would you like to count them, dear?"

"Actually, I was wondering if you would write the titles down for me." A touch of steel in Jori's voice now, as if she is used to dealing with servants. "In the order in which they were published. Please."

"Oh." Miss Hawkins looks a bit apprehensive. Is she perhaps being taken advantage of? Again? "Well. I suppose I could. Is this for a school project, dear?"

Big *aw shucks* grin from Jori. "I just want to be extra sure I don't miss a single one of them, Miss Hawkins. They're my very favourite books of all."

The librarian looks as if she might melt from relief. "Well, that's just wonderful, dear. Now, if you'll just wait for a . . . ."

"I'm afraid I have to go home now. My mother's expecting me. But I'll be back for the list this afternoon."

Brenda scuttles out behind Jori, feeling like a criminal. She knows they won't be back to the library until next Saturday, when it will be her turn to ask for something. Except Jori will have to do it, then and every time, because Brenda can never bring herself to.

"Okay," Jori says outside the library, hiking fast back along Concession Street toward Upper Wellington, with Brenda puffing along by her side. "We're covered. Now walk on ahead, just as if you're going home. Turn and wave goodbye to me. I'll meet you in five minutes. You know where."

Brenda does know where. But no matter how fast she doubles back to their meeting place under the escarpment, Jori will greet her with, "What took you so long, Brenda Bray?"

She is always there first, with the twine she filched from her mother's kitchen drawer to bind Clarence Frayne's hands behind his back, and the letter opener from her father's study that they are going to hold to his throat. She will have already spotted half a dozen clues while she was waiting for Brenda. A footprint. A broken branch. A cigarette butt. "He was just here," she will whisper. "And now he could be anywhere."

Then the two of them will stand still together, listening for the sound of breathing. For footsteps coming toward them through all the autumn crackle.

Rae

Anybody could have thrown down a cigarette butt or broken a branch. I knew that. I knew that the two of us could never tackle and subdue a grown man, too. But there I was. Going along with your crazy plan. And beginning, in my heart and against all reason, to believe in it.

God almighty. We were hunting for a serial child-killer who had escaped from the Kingston Pen, eluded police for weeks and been spotted down by the Hamilton bayfront. What in hell's name was going through our heads?

Well, we were twelve. More hormones than sense. And your plan, Jori, was exactly like you. A thin crust of brilliance over top of something essentially nuts.

Using Concession Street as an alibi was the brilliant part. If we ever needed to convince our parents that we had done exactly what every Hamilton child was being told to do in the fall of 1962, we had a string of witnesses. Yes, we had stayed together. Safety in numbers. Yes, we had stuck to a well-populated area where responsible adults could keep an eye on us. No, we had not gone anywhere near the edge of the escarpment with all its crevices and caves.

How did you ever get me to go along with you? And what made you try? What did you see, the first time you looked at me? I'm thinking back on old photographs of Brenda Bray. She was more middle-aged than I am now. Those frumpy clothes. That hair. But above all, her expression. Settled. Resigned. As if all her hope, all her curiosity, had atrophied.

Was I a challenge for you? Did you want to strike a spark in me? Ignite some passion? I couldn't even work up a half-decent fear of Clarence Frayne. I could only fear him in the abstract. On principle. When it came to something to be afraid of, it was my mother who was the clear and present danger. And my mind could go white at the thought of Annie Bray finding out what we were doing every Saturday morning.

I'm sitting writing this at a table in the Mountain Branch Public Library. It's had a lick of paint over the years. Couple of skylights put in. Computers. But even so, the second I opened the door, I got that same old whiff of books and varnish and dust. And I swear, a hint of the lily-of-the-valley perfume Miss Hawkins used to dab on her wrists.

It was like that all along Concession Street. Equal parts familiar and strange. I've just finished walking our old beat. Boone's Hobbies is a dollar store now. Same big windows, only full of cheap junk being sold cheaper. I wonder if Mr. Boone's still alive. He was maybe thirty-five when you went missing. In a way, though, he died as soon as the police started questioning him. They'd have had a field day. There wasn't much by way of gay pride in Hamilton in 1962. *Do you like kids, Boone? Which do you like better? Girls? Or boys?*

He had a complete nervous breakdown and his store was closed for almost a year. Then it was bought up by the Hobby-Time chain. They hired Mr. Boone back on to manage the business he had once owned. He spent the rest of his working days wearing the HobbyTime uniform – yellow vest, red bow tie, green checked pants.

You and I have a few things to answer for, Jori. Or maybe you wouldn't see it that way. Mr. Boone, Mr. Solly, Mrs. Slaine, Miss Hawkins. Maybe you'd regard them as so much collateral damage. You saved all your compassion for Clarence Frayne.

I used to kind of like Miss Hawkins. She might have been a bit dim, but she was a role model of sorts. What if I'd never met you, Jori? Would I have morphed into a Miss Hawkins? Found a job in this very library? Lived out my life date-stamping cards and straightening books on shelves?

It's easy to play the what-if game. What if they had found your body all those years ago? Something, anything, to put into a coffin and bury. What if there had been some kind of memorial service for you that I could have gone to, in a wheelchair if necessary? Would I have had a nervous breakdown to match my physical one? Then crawled free of the wreckage with some of the closure everybody talks about?

It's all academic. There was no closure, for anybody. Your mother overdosed on nerve pills and went into a coma not long after the police called off the search. And your father carried a torch for you till he died. Kept putting ads in the paper – *Have You Seen This Little Girl?*

Collateral damage.

Once the police had questioned her, Miss Hawkins started going a little more peculiar than she already was. She took it to heart that she was the last law-abiding adult to see you alive, and she started accosting any child that came into her library, demanding to know their name and telephone number, urging them to go straight home afterwards, then phoning the number once they'd left to make sure they did. She was transferred to the main library downtown where the other librarians could keep an

27

eye on her. Then, not long after she was put out to pasture, she had a stroke and ended up in the Home where my mother was.

Annie Bray sometimes had trouble recognizing me when I visited her in the Home. She seemed to think I was a friend of her daughter's who had come from Toronto. But Miss Hawkins always knew exactly who I was. Or maybe she just remembered who I used to be with. And somehow, in senility, the penny had finally dropped.

"No! No! No! Not again!" she would start to wail the second she saw me in the halls of the Home. She would do a complete U-turn in her wheelchair, then streak away, arms pumping, head wagging back and forth. "Never! Never! Never again!"

Yes, we do have a few things to answer for, Jori. But that's not why I'm back in a city I never wanted to see again. Writing in a diary I could never throw away, much as I wanted to.

I have nothing against the past. The past is my stock in trade. My books are set in Edwardian Toronto. My sleuth wears a bustle and stays, and has been known to defend herself with a hatpin. But as the first of the three ghosts reminds Scrooge, there is a difference between long past and one's own. The past I choose to dabble in is of the long variety. A sepia-tinted past that smells of lavender and old books. One that might lurch and scurry along in the occasional silent film, but is for the most part still.

My own past is a very different matter. All that stuff Annie Bray wouldn't let me throw out when I came home from the hospital? It was still waiting for me decades later when she went into the Home and I had to sell the house. A whole basement full of Bren-duh. I couldn't look at it. Couldn't open the boxes. Knew I'd vomit if I caught a whiff of who I used to be. So I sent it all to the dump. And I told myself that was the end of it.

I should have known better. You can't get rid of your own past. You can deny it, forget it, lie about it. But it's still *there*.

Sifting down through the landfill. Softening, rotting, shredding. But never quite gone. And here and there a filthy satin label with the words *For the Pleasingly Plump Child* still dimly visible in pink.

So, Jori, I find myself back at the scene of the crime. Playing the role of one of my own villains.

There's a part of every Elsinor Grey book that makes me cringe. I have to write it, it has to be there, but it's so damned contrived. I call it The Big Confrontation. Elsinor has finally cornered the guilty party and accused him. Melrose is, as usual, on his way. His plodding police work has finally caught up with Elsinor's intuition, and he's as frantic and furious with her as ever. Time and again, he has asked her to please stay home and just make up murder mysteries in her pretty little head. But no, there she is, endangering her life once more. So what happens? Does the murderer do the sensible thing? That is, does he simply kill the one person who possesses proof of his guilt, and then disappear? Of course not. Oh, he'll get around to it. But first, he has to deliver his big long speech about why he murdered his victim and how clever he was in fooling everybody. Everybody except Elsinor Grey, of course. Who happens to be his favourite author. But whom he is now, much to his regret, compelled to . . . At which point John Melrose bursts in with loaded pistol, police backup and cuffs.

Well. Nothing like that's going to happen today. But I am, in effect, going to deliver my big long speech. Finish the story. Set the record straight. Oh, all right, I'll say it. I want to confess, Jori. I didn't think I would ever need to, let alone want to. Then a dog found a bone. Did I mention that it happened in the first week after Labour Day? Practically the anniversary of when we met.

The first thing I had better confess to is pretension. Putting myself in the role of villain, that is. When it comes to your disappearance and probable murder, I am not, in fact, guilty.

But neither am I innocent. I fall into that in-between greyness called *culpable*. So I'm more like one of my own minor characters who's there to advance the plot. The maid who knows she shouldn't have told the lie about where the young master really was that night, but . . . Or the caretaker who knows he shouldn't have accepted the bribe to keep the door unlocked but . . . An enabler, as I'd probably be called today.

Which brings me back to Concession Street. And what I helped you do to those people. Solomon Kandinsky got a visit from the police too. The boys in blue knew what they were doing. Little girl goes missing? Standard procedure. First give Boone, the local pervert, a going-over. Then check out Kandinsky. The foreigner. The Jew. *So when exactly did you get off the boat, Solomon? Papers all in order, are they?*

Mr. Solly stopped trying to be the friendliest guy on the street. I never saw the gap between his teeth again. He took to wearing a yarmulke in the store, and he expanded his deli section. Turned himself into a Jew's Jew. My mother told me not even to buy bottled pop from him any more. He went bankrupt just months before North Americans raised on Wonder Bread started developing a taste for garlic. Solly's Variety is a big, expanded gourmet and specialty foods place now. And no, they didn't hire him on as manager. He'd gone back to the old country.

Slaine's Notions and Dry Goods is a lingerie store now called *Ooh La!* Heart-shaped bustiers in the window. Cruel little lace thongs that had me pressing my thighs together. I could just see the look on Mrs. Slaine's face.

Mrs. Slaine went on selling her notions and dry goods until 1970, when, according to a letter I got at school from my mother, she had a stroke while colour-sorting skeins of embroidery thread. But for eight years before that, she managed to hold her head up and carry on and maintain her pride. Despite the fact that police officers had pushed open her door that went *ding* and invaded her lavender-scented world in their big clumping boots. *So what about your husband, Mrs. Slaine? Do you know where he was when the girl disappeared? Home with you, was he? Does he come home every night, Mrs. Slaine?*

The last time I was in her store, waiting for Annie Bray to make her mind up about buttons or whatever, I got that spooky feeling you get when somebody's staring at you. I turned to look at Mrs. Slaine. For once in her life, she was managing to focus, and she was giving me the evil eye. Two of them.

I'll have to move on soon. It's almost eleven, and I've got a few more sites to visit before the day is out. I can't shake the feeling that you'll be travelling with me, Jori. Not that I think your spirit or ghost or whatever is literally reading over my shoulder. I've never been a believer, as far as that kind of thing goes. Just as well. The thought of Sunday lunch in Eternity with my mother and grandmother is more than I can bear.

But I have to ask. Did you drop in on my mother in the Home just before she died? She said you did. Actually, what she said was, "That (pause) Jori was here." The pause was to give her time to wrinkle up her face the way a kid does at food they don't like.

"Oh?" I said in that neutral tone I had learned to take with her. "She was? That's nice." It would never have occurred to me to say, *that's not possible*. My mother's dementia made all things possible. And for the first time in our lives, it made them almost pleasant.

One week it might be, "Your grandmother was just here, but she couldn't stay." So I would know that I was me, and I would say something like, "Oh? That's too bad. How is Granny these days?" Then the next week I'd hear, "I don't think you ever met my late husband, Art Bray. He was a Transit Operator for the Hamilton Street Railway Company. He died in the line of duty. This is the medal they gave him posthumously." So, whoever I was supposed to be, I would admire the button she had torn off her sweater. Just as if I didn't keep my father's gold medal in its velvet-covered box in the top drawer of my dresser. The people who ran the Home had warned me not to let my mother have any valuables she could lose or give away or swallow, then accuse them of stealing.

So I guess I shouldn't have been as stunned as I was, Jori, when she said you had dropped in. God knows, you had made quite an impression on her all those years ago.

I don't trust that girl. She's too nice. "Brenda tells me you're an avid reader, Mrs. Bray. Who are you favourite authors?" *So she thinks I have nothing to do all day but sit and read? Maybe her own mother can do that. Probably has servants. Mrs. Professor Clement.* "Brenda tells me you're a fan of old movies, Mrs. Bray. My parents let me watch *Random Harvest* last Saturday night, and I confess I cried myself to sleep." *Who does she think she is, with that hoity-toity talk? And what else have you been telling her about me?*

I would endure Annie Bray's rhetoric after one of your visits while choking down supper. Then the next day at school, I would listen to your analysis of her. *She is fantastic, Brenda! She is a classic case of the depressive personality. My mother did a minor in psychology, and she lets me read her old textbooks. So you say your mother hardly ever goes out of the house? And has absolutely no friends? Interesting. Interesting.*

I kept waiting for my mother to put her foot down. I used to walk on eggs every time you and I did our homework together in my room. There I was, stuck between two defining relationships who were sizing each other up. I could sense that Annie Bray was getting ready to issue an ultimatum. I think I was even hoping she

32

would. *There's something not normal about that girl. She's sick. That's what she is. Sick.*

I was cutting her hair in the Home when she said your name. Standing behind her. Looking at her in the mirror. I was working around one of her ears, using the sharp new barber's shears I'd bought. I went perfectly still. Good thing too, otherwise I might have snipped flesh along with hair. Her ears had gotten large in old age, like a monkey's.

Cutting her hair was one of our rituals. Eating grapes was another, from a Tupperware container I'd bring with me from Toronto. Then there was looking at old photographs. When I sold the house, I salvaged the ones that had hung framed in the hall between the living room and the kitchen for as long as I could remember. Annie Bray with the mayor, accepting my father's posthumous medal. Art Bray in his Hamilton Street Railway Company uniform, being awarded Transit Operator of the Year for the fifth time in a row. (I still think of him as a Transit Operator, Jori. Never, God forbid, a bus driver.)

Sometimes Annie Bray and I would take a walk outside around the Home, me pushing her wheelchair. But she put a stop to that the day she decided that if she went out, she wouldn't remember how to get back in. "I'll remember," I kept telling her. "I'll get you back in." But she dug in her heels. Literally. Planted both her Velcro-tab slippers flat on the broadloom and set the brakes on both her back wheels. So that was that. No more walks.

Then one week she was complaining about how long her hair was getting. She refused to let the hairdresser in the Home touch it because she was convinced she had already made an appointment at a salon on Concession Street, one that she hadn't been inside for over twenty years. On impulse I said, "Do you want me to cut your hair?" Her face brightened, as if I had suggested a

33

shopping trip, or lunch downtown. The kind of mother-daughter thing we had never done. So I borrowed a pair of scissors from the front desk.

After that, once a month or so, I would bring my own shears and a towel to drape over her shoulders. I knew the ritual couldn't last. She was starting to look forward to it. One day when I arrived at the Home with my equipment, she would refuse to let me cut her hair. Would deny that I had ever cut it. Would insist that she had an appointment at that salon that turned into a Blockbuster Video a decade ago.

The Home was brand new. A showcase. It had that aggressively cheerful decor that makes people who don't have to live there say, *Lovely!* My father's pension stretched just far enough to pay for a lovely room that my mother shared with a lovely, balding old lady who was just this side of catatonic. Mrs. Pasquale sat all day smiling into the sunshine, occasionally humming a tune that sounded vaguely like *Downtown*.

"You've got to watch that one," my mother would whisper if she caught me looking at her. "She's a Nosy Parker." Mrs. Pasquale was probably about as nosy as the Buddha, whom she resembled. But my mother's paranoia needed fresh meat.

"What did Jori have to say when she dropped in?" I kept my eyes on what I was doing and tried to will away the flush that had started rising in my face.

"Oh. Well. What did she *ever* have to say? Just walked in that door. Sat herself down in that chair. Said, Yes Mrs. Bray and No Mrs. Bray to me. Just the way she used to. Just as if butter wouldn't melt in her mouth."

"How did she look?" I was separating a lock of hair, pulling it straight between my fingers and snipping the ends. What was I hoping to hear, Jori? Against all reason? That you were middle-aged like me? That you couldn't stay long because your husband was waiting for you in the car? That the two of you were expecting your first grandchild in June?

"How did *who* look?" My mother was checking herself out in the mirror. "Don't make it too short," she had fussed when I started. "Don't give me bangs. I don't want bangs."

I didn't answer. Just put down my shears and started combing and styling to distract her. It worked. In less than a minute, it was as if she had never said your name. That's one of the advantages of senile dementia. You never have to change the subject. Just wait a few seconds and it changes itself.

Two days after that, Annie Bray was dead. I woke up for no reason at all just after midnight. Five minutes later, the phone rang. It was the Home. *Peacefully in her sleep.* I put the phone down and stood waiting in the dark. For tears. Guilt. Rage. Relief. Something. All I got was a strangled feeling, as if someone was pressing their thumb hard against my windpipe. And all I could think was, I'll never have to make that trip to Hamilton again.

Never say never.

Brenda

"**L**ook at that face! You look at it!" Annie Bray's finger is pressing down so hard on the photograph of Clarence Frayne that the nail is turning white. "That is the face of a monster!"

Clarence Frayne's eyes are big and bewildered, as if he can't understand what he's doing on the front page of the *Hamilton Spectator*. His mouth makes Brenda think of the Gerber Baby on the can of condensed milk her mother puts in her coffee.

"If you see anybody who looks anything like that, you come right home her and you tell me! Do you hear me? Do you?"

It is Saturday morning. Annie Bray's hair is still pin-curled flat to her head like a bristling bathing cap to preserve her perm. The smells of bacon and syrup hang sweet in the air from breakfast. Brenda glances at the kitchen clock. How soon can she get away?

"He's not even human," her mother goes on, more to herself now. She has turned the paper back around to face her, and her eyes are fixed on the front page while she sips the last of her coffee. She has been following the Clarence Frayne story for weeks now, ever since he escaped. Just the way Jori has.

"And you know what they should do when they catch him? You know what I'd do? I'd put him in a room with those five girls' mothers. There. That's what I'd do. Those poor, poor mothers."

Brenda has a sudden image of the five mothers, led by her own, descending like screeching birds on Clarence Frayne. She can feel their fingernails tearing chunks of his flesh, as if they were being torn out of her own plump arms.

She looks again at the clock. She'd better make her move. Annie Bray is working herself up into one of her rages. And once she starts, it will be all the harder to get permission to leave.

"Um, I have to go and meet Jori now? At the library? To do homework?"

"Didn't you just do homework with her? Here? Last Thursday?"

"This is a project. We have to do it together. We're partners. It's on the Aztecs."

"You see too much of that girl. It's not healthy."

She's looking at her paper again. And she hasn't exactly said no. Brenda almost wishes she would. The Saturday morning expeditions with Jori are getting spookier all the time. Not that she really thinks they're going to catch Clarence Frayne. And even if they did, she knows deep down that all he would do is give her one quick look, then go after Jori. She herself would be left alive to explain it all to the police. And to her mother. And that would be worse than being put down for a nap. Which is what Clarence Frayne said he did. 'LITTLE GIRLS LOOKED TIRED' KILLER CLAIMS was the headline in the *Spectator* when he was caught. PUT THEM DOWN FOR A NAP.

Brenda wonders if that's all he did to them. Maybe they don't put that other kind of thing in the paper. For the sake of the girls' mothers. She worked up the nerve once to ask Jori what she thought. Jori gave her a long, scary look, then said, "No. He wouldn't." And Brenda knew better than to ask how she could be so sure.

*

"Isn't he beautiful?" Jori was running her fingertips over Clarence Frayne's photograph. She had clipped every article about him from the *Spectator*, and a few from *The Globe and Mail*, which her father reads. She had glued the articles into her scrapbook, alongside other ones with headlines like HUMAN HEAD FOUND INSIDE STURGEON.

Brenda supposed she could see how somebody might think Clarence Frayne was beautiful. With those big, innocent eyes and the sweet mouth and that lock of dark hair falling over his forehead, he could be a singer with a name like Johnny or Bobby – the kind girls screamed and cried over at concerts.

"Do your parents know you keep this scrapbook?" she asked, the first time Jori showed it to her. This was before the Clarence Frayne story had broken. They had just finished reading a clipping with the headline SPINSTER RECLUSE CRUSHED BY MEMORABILIA, EATEN BY CATS.

"Of course they do. Daddy even tells me if there's anything I might want for it in the *Globe*, and hands it over to me when he's done."

"They think it's okay?"

"They think it's – what did I hear Mummy call it to Daddy? *A normal pubescent phase.*" Jori let out a high-pitched giggle. "Oh yes, and she also called it *a safe outlet for my confused adolescent fantasies.*"

Brenda wondered now if they still thought it was normal and safe. "Um, Jori? What are we going to do with Clarence Frayne if – when we find him and tie him up?"

38

Jori took a while to answer. She gazed down at the latest photograph, running her fingertips lightly over the mouth. All the mouths in the photographs were blurred, where her fingers had smudged the ink.

"He'll be so scared," she said softly at last. "There'll be a patch of damp on the back of his shirt. And maybe he'll have wet himself. Poor baby. He'll be so scared. So I'll just run my hand up and down his spine. Right from his neck to his waist. Up and down. Saying, *It's all right. You're safe.* Over and over, until I feel all his muscles relax. Has anyone ever done that for you, Brenda? Rubbed your back like that? My father does it for me in the night, if I have a nightmare and can't get back to sleep. It's the most wonderful feeling. Sometimes I even pretend to have a nightmare, just so he'll come to my room and do it. And when he does, I fight sleep for as long as I can, because I want it to go on forever."

Brenda looked at Jori's rapt face. She wished she could say in a mean voice, *My father's dead, remember?* But she didn't want to pick a fight. Jori had changed. Ever since the Clarence Frayne story had made the front page of the *Spectator*, something had come over her – a strangeness that frightened Brenda. But she wasn't sure whether she was afraid of Jori or afraid for her.

She didn't really believe they were going to capture Clarence Frayne. But she could tell that Jori did. So she tried not to ask too many questions. What exactly were they going to do with him once his muscles had relaxed? And why did Jori want her to be there? To sit on him and hold the letter opener to his throat while his hands were being tied with the twine? She knew without having to ask that Jori would do the stroking afterwards.

"Aren't you scared that he'll put us down for a nap before we can get him to lie on his stomach?" It was another dangerous question, but she had to ask it.

Again, Jori took her time answering. "No," she said softly at last. "Not us."

Brenda was sure that what she really meant to say was, *No. Not me.*

*

Brenda crosses Brucedale and takes a shortcut through Inch Park. Not that she wants to get to Concession Street any faster. She just wants to be sure not to bump into any of the other girls from school. So far this year, nobody has picked on her, maybe because she's with Jori. But what if she and Jori stop being friends? Stop walking together in line and sitting together through recess?

For the first few days of Grade Seven, before Jori came up to her and started to talk, Brenda was so alone she might as well have been invisible. She liked it. Everything at Sir Isaac Brock was new and strange – the teachers, the subjects, most of the faces in her home room class. Hardly anybody remembered her from public school. Her old nicknames. The jokes she used to be the butt of. The games.

*

"Move, Brenda."

Three girls. Always three. Arms linked, like skaters. They'd herd her all over the schoolyard all through recess. She'd be settled down in a quiet corner with her book. She always brought a book to read, then sat by herself and hoped the others wouldn't notice her. A book was a safe, secret room where she could shut the door and be alone. Once inside that room, she could be Nancy Drew or Jo March or Jane Eyre.

Her favourite parts in *Jane Eyre* were when Jane's cousins are mean to her, and when she gets sent to that awful school. People are mean to Oliver Twist and David Copperfield too. Brenda's books fell open to the mean parts, because she read them over and over.

But some days, a book wasn't enough. Some days she couldn't find the door to the safe, secret room, or she couldn't close it tightly enough behind her. Instead of the page, she would see the playground as if from very high up, full of the tiny figures of laughing, playing children. Off to one side, she would see herself. The fat girl all alone with her book. She hated seeing herself that way. There was something shameful about the distance between herself and the others. Something dirty and embarrassing and all her fault. And that's when a shadow would fall across the page.

"Move, Brenda. We want to be here, and you're taking up too much room."

So Brenda would move. And move. What else could she do? If she tried to chase the girls away, they would dance in front of her, laughing at how slow she was. She couldn't insult them back, either. What could she say to them that would hurt? Their thighs didn't chafe when they walked. Their stomachs didn't wobble when they ran.

"Move again, Brenda. We've decided we want to be here now instead. And you're still taking up too much room."

The games didn't happen every day. The girls might leave her alone for weeks. Then there'd be something like a shift in the wind, and they would catch her scent.

"Pick a number, Brenda."

A girl was offering to tell her fortune with one of those folded paper cones that fit over the fingers and went open-close. Pick a number, the fortune teller said. Pick a word. Open-close, open-close. And then your fortune, written on a point of paper unfolded. You will marry a garbage man and have ten children. Always something silly. But the fortune wasn't what mattered. What mattered was somebody coming up to you, paper cone snug and ready, saying, "Pick a number. Pick a word."

Brenda couldn't believe it was happening to her. She picked six. Open-close-open-close-open-close, counting up to six. Then, "Pick a word." Daringly, Brenda picked PRETTY from the words pencilled onto folds of the cone. PRETTY. NICE. SWEET. CUTE. Open-close-open-close, the cone went, spelling out P-R-E-T-T-Y. The other girls who had followed the fortune teller over to where Brenda was sitting were as quiet and solemn as they ever were when a fortune was being told.

"Now pick another number, Brenda."

Whatever number she chose, that part of the paper cone would be unfolded to reveal her fortune. She didn't care what it was. For once, she would be laughing along with the other girls.

She chose the number three. The girl holding the cone unfolded the part marked three. Then she read out Brenda's fortune in a loud, carrying voice. "You will get fatter and fatter until you won't be able to get out through the door of your own house." The other girls screamed, just as if they hadn't known what was written under the folds of the cone, hadn't helped make up the fortunes themselves. Then one of them said, "Read all the others."

Brenda sat perfectly still, staring at the open book in her lap. The words on the page were just mute black marks, but she stared at them anyway. Pretending not to hear.

Someday you'll eat so much you'll blow up

If you ever get married, your wedding dress will be a circus tent

Your children will be even fatter than you, and your grandchildren will be even fatter than them, and your great-grandchildren . . .

"Hop aboard, Miss Bray!"

Her father's bus. Just in time. Her father holding up his hand when the three girls try to get on behind Brenda. "Sorry, ladies. You'd take up too much room." Then driving up, up and away while the girls watch from the ground, their mouths open in astonishment and envy. And Brenda watching them from the bus window as they get tinier and tinier and . . . .

But that was last year in public school. This year in junior high, nobody was paying any attention to her. And with any luck, that was the way things would stay. She would be able to relax and read her book at recess. Nobody would be watching her, waiting to pounce. Waiting to –

"What a pathetic gathering."

The red-haired girl was just there. All of a sudden. Sitting beside her. Talking to her as if they had known each other for years.

"Look at them," The girl gestured with her chin at a group of girls clustered just a few feet away. "Not a single solitary cerebellum between them."

Brenda wished she would pipe down. She doubted any of the girls knew what cerebellum meant. But they would know they were being made fun of. And they would think Brenda was in on it.

"Do you suppose they have the slightest inkling how ridiculous they are?"

"Shhhh! They'll hear you!"

The girl gave her a *so what?* look, but she did lower her voice. "Lemmings," she murmured. "Sheep."

Brenda barely knew who she was. She had noticed her because of her red hair and because of the way she answered questions in class. If a teacher called on her, she didn't scramble to her feet the way Brenda did and answer breathlessly, as if her life depended on it. Instead, she would first give the teacher a long, cool

43

look, as if she was wondering if they could possibly be serious. Then, when she answered the question, she would always manage to sound as if she thought it was stupid.

"Jori Clement." The girl put her hand out. Brenda looked at it. Did girls shake hands? Was this a joke? A new brand of teasing? The hand didn't go away. After a second, she took it. It was slender and cold. It made her own feel hot and big.

"And you are?"

"Pardon?"

"Sorry. I really should know your name by now."

"Oh. Brenda Bray."

"Well, Brenda Bray, I've been watching you open your book each day, far from the madding crowd, and I've been meaning to tell you what a positive relief it is to know that someone around here besides me has a modicum of intelligence. What are you reading?"

She took the book out of Brenda's hands. It was *Jane Eyre*. She had been rereading the part where Jane has to eat burnt porridge for breakfast at Lowood Academy.

"You read the Brontës." It sounded like an accusation. Jori narrowed her eyes. 'Have you read *Wuthering Heights* yet?"

Brenda nodded. She thought of saying, *twice*, then didn't. What if this was a trap?

"Which is your favourite subject in school?" The narrowed eyes didn't blink.

"English?"

"Which do you like better, spring or fall?"

"Fall?"

"Which do you hate more, summer or winter?"

"Summer?"

Jori smiled and let out a deep breath, like a teacher whose pupil had just passed a crucial exam. "Brenda Bray," she said crisply, handing *Jane Eyre* back to her, "I believe this may be the beginning of – oh, *merde!*"

The bell was clanging for the end of recess. They had to run and line up, girls in front of the GIRLS entrance, boys in front of the BOYS. And there was no talking in line.

Gym class was right after recess. The blue uniform they all had to wear had bloomer bottoms that made Brenda's hips look wider, and cap sleeves that fluttered above her fat arms like little wings. In the locker room, she always got changed as quickly as possible, hating the moment of having nothing on but her underwear. But this day, she took her time and watched Jori out of the corner of her eye.

Jori's hair was cut in a pageboy, and she still wore the sort of clothes everybody had worn up until the end of grade six – cotton blouses, plaid skirts, saddle shoes and socks. The kind Brenda still wore. The two of them were starting to look like children compared to the rest. All the other girls were shortening their skirts and taking them in to make them tighter. Wearing nylon stockings and hard little pointed bras. Teasing their hair to the texture of candy floss, then molding it into the shape of beehives. At recess they all stood together in circles of five or six, whispering and giggling and sometimes passing around a cigarette. Last week Brenda had heard one of them say *fuck* when she pulled a run in her nylon.

Jori was already into her gym uniform, lacing up her shoes. Brenda had thought she was skinny, but now she saw that she was lean and muscled, her skin pale but without the freckles that so often come with red hair. She wore a cotton undershirt just like Brenda's and didn't have even the beginnings of breasts. Her face was not pretty, Brenda decided. It was too heart-shaped, with its wide forehead, small mouth and pointed chin. Her nose was big, too, and slightly hooked. And her eyes were oddly far apart. From a distance, with their pale lashes, they looked like green peas floating in –

She was looking straight at Brenda. Brenda turned away, a hot blush spreading up from her throat.

In gym class they all had to run in turn and jump onto a leather-covered vaulting horse. Each time Jori jumped, the teacher barked, "Nice!" at the way she landed perfectly poised, one leg bent, the other extended. The third time Brenda came lumbering up to the horse and crashed into it, the teacher rolled her eyes and said something about damaging school property that made the rest of the class laugh. Brenda felt a familiar pang. That was the end of being invisible. Now the nicknames would start. And maybe the games.

After gym, Brenda got dressed as fast as she could, keeping her eyes down. She felt a touch on the back of her neck and turned around. The touch was Jori, tucking the label inside the collar of her blouse for her. "All set now," she said, giving Brenda a conspiratorial smile. The smile lingered, as if daring her to look away first. She did, blushing again. She wondered if Jori had seen the words *Pleasingly Plump* stitched in pink.

On the way home that day, Brenda heard running steps behind her. "I waited for you!" Jori sounded as if she thought they had made some arrangement to meet and walk home together. "Why are you in such a hurry?"

"I don't know." Brenda's voice sounded gruff and stupid to her own ears.

"Well then, slow down. Let's get acquainted."

Brenda stiffened. This had to be a trap. Well, she wasn't going to fall into it. She walked in silence beside Jori for half a block, feeling the other girl's eyes on her. Keeping her own fixed straight ahead.

Finally Jori said, "Do you have any other names besides Brenda Bray?"

"No. Just Brenda."

"Well, Just Brenda, consider yourself lucky. I've got three names, and I don't particularly like any of them. Marjorie's for my Aunt Marjorie, my mother's sister. She lives in Toronto and says I can live with her when I go to U of T. I like everything about my aunt except her name, which sounds like margarine. That's why I insist on Jori. Then I'm Susannah for my mother and Victoria for my father, whose name is Victor. There. Marjorie Susannah Victoria Clement. But what about you, Brenda Bray? Who are you named for?"

It was hard to ignore somebody when they asked you questions. "I'm not named after anybody." Then, because Jori was still looking at her, she added, "My mother's named Anne Louise. And my father was called Art."

"Was? Is your father dead?"

She nodded.

"When did he die?"

"Long time ago. When I was a baby."

"Do you visit his grave?"

Brenda wanted to tell her to mind her own business. But then she thought, *Maybe if I tell her what she wants to know, she'll go away and leave me alone.* "Yes. We do visit his grave. My mother and I. On Father's Day."

"What do you do there? Do you weep and sing hymns? Read Bible verses?"

Brenda looked at Jori to see if she was making fun of her. But she was giving her the same narrow, assessing look she had when she was asking all those questions at recess.

Carefully, Brenda said, "We just stand there for a moment. Then we go home." What she didn't say was that her mother sometimes told her stories about her father. About how Art Bray could greet most of his passengers by name, and ask after their husbands and children. About how she didn't like him at first, thought he was a show-off. Then one day she got on his bus with a bandaged ankle. When it was time for her to get off, he went down the steps before her and reached up a steadying hand. After that, whenever she got on his bus, he asked about her ankle.

"Do you think about your father?"

"I told you. He died when I was a baby. I don't remember him." She would never tell anyone about her bus daydreams.

"No." Jori caught her arm and made her stop walking. "That's not what I mean." Her mouth was small and pale, her green eyes fixed unblinking on Brenda's face. "I mean, do you try to imagine him. Now. In his coffin."

Brenda's mouth went dry. Could this girl read her thoughts? Was she one of those people who have ESP?

"Don't mind me," Jori said all of a sudden, tucking her arm into Brenda's and starting to walk. She was all breezy and confident again, the way she had been at recess. "It's just that I've never known anybody who had a dead father before, and I've always wondered if that's the kind of thing that would go through one's mind. My mother says I have an overactive imagination, and that I dwell on things most people would rather not even think about. But then Daddy says, Well, Suzie, at least the girl is thinking. And that stops Mummy in her tracks, because she hates it when Daddy calls her Suzie, and because she can't exactly contradict him, can she? Honestly, Brenda Bray, I wonder sometimes about those two. I mean, they're intelligent enough. Mummy has her Master's in French literature, and Daddy is all Latin and Greek – he's Professor of Classical Studies at McMaster. But they've already started bickering like children about who's going to tutor me when I start taking languages in high school. If they'd

48

stop and use their heads for a minute, they'd realize that I simply won't need a tutor. In languages or anything else. And I don't think I'm being conceited, saying that. I'm just being realistic. Do you think I'm being conceited?"

"No," Brenda said after a second. Then, because it occurred to her that as long as Jori talked about herself she wouldn't ask any more strange questions, she added encouragingly, "You're really good in gym, too."

Jori sighed. "That's my father's influence again. He takes this *mens sana in corpore sano* thing just a bit too far, quite frankly. It almost makes me wish I had siblings. I mean, to give my parents something besides me to think about. Daddy especially. But no, they just wanted the one. I was a planned child and a wanted child. Or so I've been told, since before I could have had the slightest inkling what they were talking about. What about you, Brenda Bray? Do you have siblings?"

"No." Brenda knew she sounded stupid, but the one word was all she could manage. She had given up on trying to make Jori go away. She could only hope she lived nearby, so they could separate soon. It was embarrassing to walk along the street arm-in-arm. She winced at the sight of their shadows stretching in front of them – Jori's narrow and straight, her own lumpy and wide.

Jori had just asked her another question. "Pardon?"

"I said, are you sure you have no siblings?"

"How could you not be sure about something like that?"

"Because you can have a twin and not know it. I keep a scrapbook about things like this. And there's a newspaper clipping in it that I'll let you see, about a man in the States who was hanged for murder. And they donated his body to science. And when some medical students cut him open, they found this weird lump inside. And when they cut the lump open, they found hair

49

and teeth and bits of bone." Jori paused, still looking at Brenda intently. "It was the man's twin! He had eaten his own twin! Before they were born! The headline is MURDER STARTS IN THE WOMB. It's one of my favourite clippings. But you'll see all of them, Brenda Bray, when you come to visit."

Suddenly they jerked to a halt. "That's my house," Jori said, pointing. "That one. There." Brenda, still wondering what Jori meant about coming to visit, looked and saw a fieldstone cottage perching on the edge of the escarpment. She knew the house. She and her mother walked past it every Sunday morning on their way to church. Strange to think that Jori had been living in it all the time.

"I'd ask you in today," she was saying, "but Mummy and I have an appointment to go and talk with my new ballet teacher. I'll be doing a lot more toe work this year, or so I'm told. That's another thing about my parents, Brenda Bray. They think I'm the Sugar Plum Fairy." She rolled her eyes. "My God. If they only knew." Then she laughed and said, "*Au revoir*," and turned and walked away.

Brenda stood on the sidewalk, watching Jori walk toward her house, her red pageboy swinging. There was that sudden absence in the air that there is when a loud, ongoing racket has finally stopped. Brenda knew there was nothing keeping her there on the corner. No reason to stand and watch Jori go. But all at once she wanted her back, for just a minute. She was ashamed of the brief, guttural answers she had given to her questions. She wished she could have a second chance. Annie Bray's voice invaded her mind: *Couldn't even put two words together. What are you, retarded?*

Jori had reached the front door of the fieldstone cottage. As if she knew that Brenda would still be standing on the corner, she turned and waved. Brenda was so flustered that she didn't wave back, just hurried away along Concession Street, hearing her mother's voice again: *Standing there waiting like a big, dumb lump. What are you, desperate? You don't need her.*

*

And there is Jori now, waiting for her outside Boone's Hobbies on Concession Street. Just the way she always does, every Saturday morning. It always surprises Brenda to see her there. She keeps expecting Jori to get tired of her. Stop wanting to be with her. *Well, so what if she does? You don't need her.*

Jori's hand comes up in a wave just as Brenda is thinking, *I don't need you.* She keeps on thinking it, even as her steps quicken and she waves back.

Rae

Here's another what-if for you, Jori. When you asked me which season I hated more, summer or winter, what if I'd said winter?

You were ahead of your time, dividing the world into summer people and winter people. It was decades before the cat person-dog person thing got started.

"Summer People never learn." You were fed up with the heat that was hanging on through the middle of that September. "Every single year, they're so excited about the days staying light till nine. And everything so green. Then they're so stricken when it starts to change. Can't they get it through their heads that all that prettiness is nothing but a cover-up? I'd like to push their faces into a full-blown rose and say, Here. Smell the rot."

You scared me when you got going like that. The Brenda Brays of this world learn early that when it comes to ridicule, they're here not to give, but to receive. And I was terrified that someday I might be on the receiving end of yours. So I kept my eyes open and made sure you had lots of targets.

"Life-sized plastic chicken in front yard," I would mutter as we walked home from school. "Plastic chicks clustered all around."

"Noted," you would answer, your lips barely moving.

"Sunglasses." This in Solly's Variety, while fishing pop out of the cooler. "Pink plastic frames with mauve sparkles."

"Noted."

It's high noon. I'm in a place called *Wellie's* on Upper Wellington. With a name like that, it should be a pub, but it's desperately trying to be a bistro. Rustic little tables. Vases full of autumn leaves. I've just finished a chicken and wild mushroom salad. Dressing on the side. Half a bun. No butter. And I've just been handed the dessert menu. Nobody ever asks me if I want to see the dessert menu. It just appears. Waiters take one look at me and assume that I have the metabolism of a hummingbird. I wish.

The fact is, nothing is easy or automatic for me. Not staying thin. Not writing mysteries. I keep trying to get back to *November Days*, the manuscript I stopped working on for a few weeks after that bone was found. It was to be the "grow old along with me" book in the series. Elsinor approaching sixty, John already retired. Elsinor still exasperated by the very stuffiness that endears John to her. John still as fascinated as he is bewildered by Elsinor's independence.

When the tests on the bone were inconclusive, I assumed I could pick up where I had left off. But I was wrong. The manuscript has a foreign feel, almost as if somebody else wrote it. The plot that was just starting to gel in my mind when I got distracted seems more contrived than ever. And something has happened to my relationship with Elsinor. There is a distance between us. A cooling of the air. I can feel it.

For years now, she's been my constant companion, walking with me through the streets of Toronto, helping me see them through her eyes. Thanks to her, all the sepia-tinted photographs that I've studied and memorized come to life and start to move, in full, fresh colour. Oh, I know I'm imagining it all. Imagining her. But imaginary beings do live, in their way. They can die, too. Or just withdraw themselves.

Once years ago at a book signing, when the line was particularly long and slow, I overheard a man telling his companion how he kept busy since his retirement. He scanned the community newspapers, he said, for coming events. Garage sales and garden tours and historical walks sponsored by the public library. Things that wouldn't eat into his fixed income. He wrote these events into the spaces on his calendar, with the result that just about every day of the month, he woke up in the morning knowing he had something to do.

Maybe he was going a bit deaf and didn't realize how loud he was talking. Because that *something to do* rang out like a bell, then reverberated in the air. I actually stopped in the middle of my own signature, my pen stuck to the page. *Something to do.* Oh God, I prayed silently to a deity in whom I'm not sure I believe, Let me never, ever become someone who needs to seek and find, each and every day, *something to do.*

Well, it could happen. I have the distinct impression that Elsinor has begun to disapprove of me, Jori. You see, there is a certain morality to murder mysteries – an ethical imperative. When someone is murdered, most of the world is indifferent. Some, especially the murderer, may rejoice. Or take some perverse pleasure in the killing. Even the mourners eventually settle for whatever story emerges about what happened and why, whether it's true or not, just for the sake of closure. But there is one person who presses on through the deceit and the complacency. Who cares enough for this dead soul, who might well be a total stranger, to find out the truth of what happened to them and to let that truth be known.

I can't do that for you, Jori. But I can finally tell the truth about my part in it. Brenda's part in it. And maybe that will appease Elsinor. Not to mention you.

What kept you so long, Brenda Bray?

Brenda seems to have caught a whiff of the old home town. She's started to assert herself. When I was walking along Upper Wellington, I kept squeezing unnecessarily over to the edge of the sidewalk to let people pass.

Upper Wellington. It used to just kill you, the way Hamilton Mountain was such an urban afterthought. Upper Wellington, Upper Wentworth, Upper this and Upper that. Remember your Upper People? *The Smiths and the Upper-Smiths.* You sounded like you were announcing them at a dress ball. *The Kringles and the Upper-Kringles.* I'm sitting here almost half a century later, trying not to giggle. I don't know why it was so funny, but it was. You made me almost wet my pants with *The Luppers and the Upper-Luppers.* I'd never laughed like that before. Full out. Hooting. Snorting. Red face. Wet cheeks. Chins quivering. It scared me. What else could you make me do? What if we were still friends by summertime? Would you want me to go swimming with you at the local pool? Would you insist on talking to me in the change room instead of turning your back? Would you see my dimpled bum? My sagging belly?

The way things turned out, it was all academic. By summer, I was skin and bones and you were still missing, presumed dead.

I dropped in on Sir Isaac Brock before I came here. Tecumseh Junior High, as it is now. Wonder when that happened. Probably in the PC eighties. Annie Bray would have sent me a clipping from the *Spectator* about it, but I never paid much attention to those. I'd just glance at them to make sure they weren't about your body being found, then trash them. Those clippings were the only thing about my mother that I missed, once she was dead. Even now sometimes when I'm opening my mail, I keep expecting to see a Hamilton postmark and her spiky little handwriting on the envelope.

The playground was empty. I walked alongside the fence, trying to pick out the spot where you found me hiding inside *Jane Eyre*. Wasn't there a storage shed or something, with a bench up against it? I think I remember a door with a steel padlock. Graffiti carved into the walls. But it's like trying to remember a dream.

Caramel-crusted Crème Brûlée. Double Double Chocolate Chocolate. Warm Cinnamon Apple Smother. Christ. I feel like a celibate reading porn. It's a constant vigil, even now. In the supermarket, everywhere I look I see the F-word. Low-Fat. No-Fat. Fat-free. Brenda clamours inside me like a junkie – *Gimme fat! Gimme fat!* The other day I saw a newspaper headline you would have loved: OBESITY ON THE RISE. It made me think of the loaves of homemade bread dough that Annie Bray used to set on top of the heat vent in the living room. They reminded Brenda of her own thighs – dimpled and white and getting bigger by the minute.

I've ordered the crème brûlée. Just so I can stay here a bit longer. I will have exactly two spoonfuls of it when it comes. No more. Then I'll take another walk to work it off.

After you disappeared, Jori, everybody just assumed I was slimming down naturally, maybe because of puberty. What they didn't know was that I would swallow the food my mother pressed on me, then, on my way to school, find a hidden spot where I could stick my finger down my throat. The gnawing in my stomach was the only thing that would stop the screaming in my head.

Breakfast and lunch were easy to get rid of. Supper was trickier. I would wait till I knew Annie Bray was asleep, then tiptoe to the bathroom. Sometimes I fell asleep before she did, and would miss my chance. Those missed chances, that bit of food I managed to keep inside me, probably saved my life. Weekends were hardest of all. I would practically beg for errands to do, anything that would get me out of the house so I could go somewhere and vomit.

My mother took me to see our family doctor, the one who had delivered both her and me and who now wore two hearing aids and walked with two canes. He patted me on the head, said something about young girls changing in the twinkling of an eye and prescribed a regimen of milkshakes between meals. The taste of my vomit got sweeter.

The day the police officially stopped looking for you, I struggled up from my desk at school to answer a question. Before I could say a word, I collapsed on the floor like a bundle of bones.

There. I've had my two spoonfuls of crème brûlée. I've savoured them. I've held them in my mouth. I've enjoyed every second of them slipping down my throat. And I've pushed the dish away. That's my big diet secret. I eat like Ivan Denisovich. I make much of next to nothing. Not the way poor Brenda used to eat. Inhaling half a loaf of buttered bread at one sitting. And the empty space inside her getting bigger and emptier.

In the hospital I kept drifting in and out of a coma. Sometimes, when I was just starting to surface, I would see Brenda's face. It was actually my mother's face, but before the features swam together into Annie Bray, they would be Brenda. Daytime. Night time. Whenever I woke up, a face was there to greet me. Brenda Bray. Annie Bray. Brenda Bray. Whichever it was, there was always the same look in the eyes. *Don't leave me.*

I remember feeling so detached. As if I'd broken away. Broken free. That silent pleading, whoever it was coming from, had nothing to do with me. *If I die, I'll do it by myself,* I thought over and over. Then at some point it changed to, *If I live, I'll do it by myself.*

And thereby hangs a tale.

Brenda

B renda is walking home from school. She's said goodbye to Jori and left Concession Street behind. She's taken Upper Wellington to Brucedale, and now she's working her way along Brucedale in a big zigzag, side street by side street. She veers off Brucedale for the length of a block, crosses at the far corner and walks back down the same block. Then she crosses Brucedale and does the same thing with the block on the other side.

"Miss Bray!" Her father has just pulled up to the curb and is calling down to her from his high driver's seat. "I've been hankering after a doughnut all afternoon. Care to join me?" She climbs up into his bus and they drive off together to a diner in Heaven.

Art Bray slings his uniform jacket across the back of his chair and sits with his elbows on the table. He rolls up his sleeves and pushes his peaked cap back on his head. And because Annie Bray isn't there to hear, he calls himself a plain old bus driver. Winking *don't tell* at Brenda.

He orders coffee for himself and Orange Crush for her. "Gotta have something to wash a doughnut down with, Miss Bray." He knows all the waitresses by name. One of them refills his cup saying, "So who's your new girlfriend, Art?" Pretending to be jealous.

"This," Art Bray announces, gesturing grandly, "is Miss Brenda Bray, one and only daughter of the bus driver's bus driver!" He drums his fingers on the table and all the waitresses applaud and Brenda's doughnut and Orange Crush are on the house.

Brucedale again. Only three zigzags left. No matter how slow she goes, sooner or later she'll be standing on the sidewalk outside her house. And there's only fourteen steps from the sidewalk to the door.

It's Thursday. She was supposed to bring Jori home with her after school today to do homework. Turn-about for going to her house on Tuesday. But then Hurricane Annie started up on Wednesday morning. It will probably take until Saturday to wear itself out. She told Jori that her mother was sick, so she couldn't visit after all. "Next Thursday for sure," she said to Jori's disappointed face, then wished she hadn't. She can't stop Thursday from coming, any more than she can forever avoid arriving home today.

*

"Which of the elements do you identify with, Brenda Bray? I think of myself as fire and water."

That left Brenda with earth and air. Not that fire and water weren't still there for the taking. But they were both so perfect for Jori, so obviously hers, that Brenda didn't think she had any claim on them. So. Air? Wind was kind of interesting. But wind belonged to Hurricane Annie. "Oh, earth I guess," she said shrugging.

They were in Jori's bedroom, sitting on the bed. Brenda had never seen a white ruffled canopy before. The second she saw the

59

one above Jori's bed, she wanted one above her own. Then she imagined the big lump of herself sleeping under it and decided she didn't want it after all. She was better off in her own bed with the wooden peg-legs that bowed outward and the broken slat that had to be propped underneath with a cinder block. There was a white satin spread on Jori's bed that she had to decide not to want, too, and a slippery heap of white satin cushions – some round, some diamond-shaped, some heart-shaped.

"I will sleep only in white," Jori told her that day. "Mummy knows better than to buy me coloured sheets. I won't sleep in them. I will sleep in white until I lose my virginity. Then I will cut out the bloodstained patch and keep it forever."

Brenda couldn't think of a single thing to say to that. Had Jori told her mother the reason she had to have white sheets? How much do you bleed when you lose your virginity? As much as you do when you have your period? Jori seemed to know about these things. Had she asked her mother? And had Mrs. Clement actually told her? Was that normal?

"You listen to me!" Annie Bray had just found Brenda's stained underpants in the clothes hamper. All Brenda knew was that the stain had come from her. It was frightening and strange. But there was something about it that she recognized. It was Other Brenda. Finally showing herself to the world. All the rottenness and nastiness that had been building up inside Brenda all her life was leaking out at last.

Sometimes Brenda wondered if everybody had a second person inside them that they had to keep hidden. Somebody who thought and felt and wanted to do all the things normal people didn't. Her own wanted to know how Art Bray looked now in his coffin. How he smelled. In church, Other Brenda looked around at the people and imagined old Mrs. McCutcheon straining on the toilet. Fat Mr. Carmichael unzipping his pants to pull out something long and rubbery to pee with. Reverend Culver picking his nose. Shifting on his chair to ease out a fart.

Worst of all, Other Brenda turned her head and looked, where Brenda was never supposed to look, at a lady sitting in a pew across the aisle. This lady had white poodle curls shining through the black dotted veil of her hat. Her face was exactly like Annie Bray's, only older and more pinkly powdered.

Brenda had never spoken to this old lady. But she knew who she was, and where she lived. She could even remember visiting her once, when she was young enough to be put down for a nap on the old lady's bed.

She remembered waking up to the sound of a high keening whine, like the sound a dog makes if it's been left alone outside a store. Under the keening was the sound of the old lady's voice. Not loud. Not even harsh. Just murmuring on and on.

" – but no, you had to get married. To your bus driver."

Brenda sucked in her breath. Transit Operator. Not bus driver. Saying bus driver was worse than saying bum. But all she heard was more keening. The old lady's soft words were bringing this sound out of her mother like a knife slowly probing this way and that, just under the skin.

"Things could have been so different, Anne Louise. You could have finished school. You were a bright girl. A good student. You could have gone to teacher's college. There's good money in teaching. Your father would still be alive. You know it was the shock that killed him. And the shame. I would still be living with him in our house on Empress Street instead of all alone inside this box."

More keening from Annie Bray. Brenda sat up on the bed, then slid her feet onto the floor. Just to make a noise. To let them both know that she was awake.

"Well well. Look who's up," Thelma Craig greeted her when she stepped into the kitchen doorway. Her mother kept her head turned away. "And isn't she getting to be a big girl. Going to take after her father. Can see that already."

That was the last time Brenda's grandmother ever spoke to her or to her mother. Thelma Craig sat a few feet away from them every Sunday morning in Knox Presbyterian, but did not turn her head in their direction. And Brenda understood that she was not supposed to look over at her. But Other Brenda did not understand. Or didn't care. Other Brenda wanted to heave herself up out of her pew and lumber across the aisle and sit in the old lady's lap and break her knees.

Other Brenda was deeper inside than Brenda's finger could go. Almost every night when she explored the strange wet terrain between her legs, she half expected to touch the tip of another finger reaching out. And now she must have broken through. Unleashed Other Brenda into the world. The stain on her underpants was proof.

"You listen!" There were tears in Annie Bray's voice. She had just given Brenda a sanitary belt and pad to wear. "If a boy starts to touch you or fool with you – you know what I mean." She gestured vaguely at Brenda's stomach. "You have to make him stop! Do you hear me? You can't let him keep doing it! Or else you'll have a baby!"

Brenda held her breath. Her mother was getting close to one of the things that was never talked about. One of the things that was never even mentioned, except on Hurricane Annie days, when it was screamed. Howled.

The sanitary belt was digging into her soft belly. The pad was starting to chafe where her thighs met. She had heard how the boys at school talked about girls. She had seen the drawings they inked into their textbooks and chalked onto walls. Her mother couldn't possibly be talking about anything that might happen to her. Who would ever want to put his hands on Brenda Bray?

And now here was Jori talking about losing her virginity as if she expected it to happen just any day now. Brenda still had only a vague idea of what made a baby, what exactly went where on a wedding night. Could she ask Jori about things like that? Was that a normal thing for girlfriends to do?

Were they even girlfriends? Jori seemed to think so. She had taken right over, insisting that they be partners in line between classes and spend recess with each other and walk home together after school. The other kids in their class probably thought they were girlfriends by now. So maybe they were. After all, Jori had invited her home. And here they were.

*

Brucedale. Just one more zigzag and she'll be at the bottom of her own street. Whenever Hurricane Annie is raging, it's hard for Brenda to believe that the good times will ever come back again. The times when they talk about the books that Brenda is reading – the same ones Annie Bray read as a girl. When they lean toward each other over the supper table, like school chums: *Have you got to the part yet where . . . Do you remember the part when . . . .*

And the times when they watch old movies together on TV. "It was always the movies, always," Annie Bray croons during commercial breaks. When she was a girl, she tells Brenda, she got ten cents allowance each week. Five cents had to go into the plate that was passed around in Sunday school. The other five cents was hers to spend. "I went all by myself, too. I didn't need anybody with me. Other girls would sit and talk and giggle and miss half the show. But I would – oh, look. Here's the part where . . . ."

Every Saturday, once Brenda and her mother have brought home the week's groceries, they look through the TV Guide and plan what movies they'll watch. Bette Davis. Joan Crawford.

Clark Gable. All the stars Annie Bray worshiped when she was growing up.

"Jezebel!" she all but moans, putting the canned goods in the kitchen cupboard while Brenda sits on the folded paper bags to flatten them. "Oh, Jezebel! Just wait till you see Bette Davis in her red dress. She was supposed to wear white, but she comes all in red, and Henry Fonda teaches her a lesson by waltzing her around for everybody to see . . ." Annie Bray waltzes around the kitchen, clutching two cans of peas. "And her eyes are just pleading with him, but no, he won't let her go."

Sometimes when they're watching TV together, sharing a bowl of Bridge Mixture, Brenda sneaks a glance at her mother. Annie Bray's expression changes to match Greer Garson's or Barbara Stanwyck's. Her lips move, silently mouthing the dialogue along with the stars. "I only tried out for the school play once," she has told Brenda over and over. "It was *The Merchant of Venice*. I know I could have played Portia. I'd practiced her mercy speech all week in my room. Then came the tryouts. I managed to get up in front of everybody. But when I opened my mouth, all that came out was a squeak. And my hands were shaking so hard that I dropped my copy of the play. Everybody laughed then. They always did. It was a big joke how nervous I was. Anyway, the night of the play, I sat there in the audience thinking how much better I would have been. The girl they picked to be Portia sounded like she didn't even understand her lines."

Brucedale again. Every step brings Brenda closer to home. While she walks the final block she thinks, *At least I managed to put Jori off. This time.* But there's always the next time. And the time after that.

*

64

"Just don't stay for supper."

That was how Annie Bray finally gave Brenda permission to go to Jori's house after school. "People only ask to be polite. They hate it when you say yes." She took the whole weekend to tell Brenda she could accept Jori's invitation.

"Clement?" she said when Brenda asked her last Friday night. "They're not Catholic, are they? Has this Jori been going to some Catholic school?"

"No. She's been going to Glenferris."

"Hoo hoo. Money. So what's she doing in a public school now?"

"Her parents want her to have a less elitist experience." That was how Jori had put it.

"They mean a less expensive experience. Don't believe everything you hear. And don't get all involved with this girl, whoever she is." The way Annie Bray said *all involved* made it sound dirty.

By Saturday, she was starting to get agitated. Brenda was afraid her mood would heat up and explode into one of her screaming fits. It could happen. Her rage was always there, like the weather. She could go from sunshine to thunderstorm in seconds. Dirty socks dropped balled into the clothes hamper, after she had told and told and told Brenda to pull them out flat. A book overdue at the Mountain Branch Public Library, where she had been going all her life, and where now, thanks to Brenda, she would never be able to hold her head up again. For the shame. Did Brenda hear her? *The shame.*

"I don't like the idea of you going to a strange house," she was starting to mutter by Saturday night while she mashed the potatoes for supper. "Who are these people, anyway? What kind of people are they? I should phone this Mrs. Clement. Where did you say the house was? Alpine Boulevard? Lah-dee-dah."

She went as far as looking the Clements up in the phone book and writing their number down on the back of an envelope which she propped against the radio on the kitchen counter. Brenda kept glancing at it all through supper. All evening, she held her breath whenever her mother got up out of her chair and headed toward the kitchen.

By Sunday, Annie Bray was playing it tiny and wistful. "Just don't be too late," she whispered between sips of tea. "Get home before the street lamps come on. Or I'll worry." Then she said what she did about not staying for supper.

Earth. That was Brenda's element, all right. What else could she possibly be?

"Earth," Jori repeated, giving Brenda that critical stare of hers over a heart-shaped cushion. Brenda had to look away. Jori really wasn't teasing her. She was serious. "Yes. I think earth is right for you, Brenda Bray. Because there's a paradox with earth, isn't there? We grow our food in the earth. But we also bury our dead in it. Yes. A paradox. Just like fire and water. Good for you."

*

Brucedale. For the last time. No more zigzags. On Hurricane Annie days Brenda stops for a moment at the bottom of her own street and wishes she could disappear. Cease to exist. It would be the perfect time for Art Bray to come rattling up in his death-bus and take her away.

Where else could she go? To Thelma Craig's? The thought almost makes her laugh. Her grandmother's face would change when she saw who it was. And if she didn't just slam the door, she would join forces for once with Annie Bray and send Brenda straight back home where her mother was probably worried sick about how late she was. *A big girl like you.*

She couldn't turn to any of the neighbours either. She has never knocked on any of their doors, and according to Annie Bray none of them are normal anyway. The Simpsons are loud. The Tonks are stuck-up. The Bouteliers are French. Then there are the Abrams, those Jews who can't talk about anything except money. And the Woiczas, those foreigners who don't know how to keep clean. And finally their next door neighbours, the Powells, who broadcast everything you tell them, so don't for God's sake tell them anything.

Brenda walks slowly up her street toward her house, listening to the neighbourhood children calling to each other, starting up some pre-supper game. She can't imagine being part of that ragged swarm, all different ages and sizes. One year they built dirt forts in an empty lot on the street and played war. Then they put on a circus in one of their backyards, and charged admission. And last summer they decided they needed a song to sing at the end of the day before they were all called in to bed.

Brenda found out about the song one afternoon when she was coming home from the drugstore with a bottle of headache pills for her mother. Annie Bray's screaming fits gave her a lot of headaches. Without thinking, Brenda paused in front of the Bouteliers' where Sandra Boutelier and Karin Woicza were sitting on the front porch singing softly together. They were trying out lines of *Day is Done, Gone the Sun.* Looking into each other's eyes while they sang, smiling a little. Sandra had ugly hair, chopped at cheekbone level and pulled back on top. Karin's left eye wandered off to the side. But the sight and sound of them, singing together when day was almost done and soon would be gone the sun, stopped Brenda and made her stare.

"Should we sing *amen* at the end?" Karin said to Sandra, then sang it.

"Maybe a-*men*," Sandra sang back, making the second note higher than the first.

Then the two girls saw Brenda on the sidewalk, and their faces changed. "What are you looking at, Bren-duh?" one of them asked. And the other said, "Yeah, mind your own beeswax, Bren-duh." Then added as an afterthought, "You're so darned fat."

Now at last Brenda is standing on the sidewalk outside her own house, looking at the drawn drapes. Wishing she hadn't zigzagged after all. Wishing she had already been home for an hour, so the worst would be over.

Could she turn around right now and go to Jori's house?

What a thought. Almost as stupid as going to Thelma Craig's or imagining her father coming for her in his bus. But what if she did? Would Mrs. Clement smile when she opened the door and saw who it was? Would she let her in? Let her stay?

*

Mrs. Clement was sitting reading in a wing chair in the living room on Tuesday when Jori introduced Brenda to her. She looked as if she might be expecting company. She wasn't wearing a house dress, and her stockings weren't rolled down to her ankles the way Annie Bray's usually were, to keep them from snagging. The living room looked ready for company too. There were even fresh flowers in a vase on one of the little tables that seemed to be everywhere.

Mrs. Clement lowered her reading glasses when Jori introduced Brenda, letting them hang from a silver chain. She stood up, extended her hand and said, "I'm very pleased to meet you, Brenda. Marjorie – sorry – Jori has told me so much about you."

Brenda mumbled a *How do you do* to Mrs. Clement, worrying that her hand might be sweaty. Mrs. Clement's hand was as cool and dry as Jori's was. She was wearing a pale grey dress, with a very tiny print pattern, and her earrings were little silver shells. Her dark hair was pulled smooth into a knot at the nape of her neck, and her lipstick was neither the Poppy Red nor the Coral Pink that Annie Bray wore, but something more the colour of real lips.

A word came into Brenda's mind. Taste. They were starting to learn about taste at school in Home Ec. Good taste did not depend on money, their teacher said. It was a matter of judgement. Sometimes in Home Ec Brenda would do a mental tour of her own house, trying to find something that was in good taste. For the first time, she saw how the wine satin brocade couch in the living room clashed with the pink flowered nylon drapes.

Good taste had to do with smallness, like the print of Mrs. Clement's grey dress, and with subtlety, like the colours of the flowers in this room. Russet and wine and cream. None of the red or yellow or orange that Annie Bray would have picked out. Good taste had something to do with time, too. Everything in this room looked as if it had been there for ages. The brass of the lamps had darkened. The cushions of the chairs were dented, and the carpet was worn. All at once Brenda regretted the shiny turquoise blouse Annie Bray had gotten for her last week on sale at Kresge's, and hoped it was still tucked into the back of her brown skirt.

"Mar – Jori, when your father gets home, be sure to bring Brenda in to meet him. And perhaps we'll have a little something."

"Don't get too excited," Jori muttered to Brenda as soon as they were out of the living room. "The little something will be lemonade while they sip their sherry. They like to think they're so modern and avant-garde. But deep down, they are so bloody bourgeois."

Brenda had no idea what Jori was talking about. She felt as if she had just stepped into a story where everything was right. Everything was the way things should be. The way they should always have been.

*

Brenda opens the side door, inhaling the scent of her house, sensing her mother's waiting presence. As long as one of her hurricanes lasts, Annie Bray won't wash or get dressed in the morning. She won't open the drapes or answer the door or do any housework. She will stay in her nightgown the whole time, with only her fraying orange housecoat over top. A stale smell will waft from her whenever she moves in on Brenda.

Brenda can usually tell when a hurricane is building. If things have been sunny between the two of them for a while, she starts bracing herself.

*

Professor Clement stood up when Jori led Brenda back into the living room, just as if they were ladies. Jori said, "Daddy, this is my friend, Brenda Bray. Brenda, this is my father, Professor Victor Clement." Brenda almost missed his outstretched hand, because she turned to look at Jori. There was a sweet girlishness in her tone that Brenda had never heard before. She half-expected her to drop a curtsy.

"So this is the young lady I've heard so much about. The one who believes we old folks should be put out of our misery."

"Daddy!" Jori said, mock-sternly. Then to Brenda, "I told him about our English teacher reading your euthanasia essay out loud to the class. That's what he's going on about." She rolled her eyes at her father, then smiled demurely while he cupped her face with his hands and kissed her three times – left cheek, right cheek, left again. Brenda looked away, embarrassed. Was that what fathers and daughters did? Was it normal? Would her own father do it to her if he was alive?

When they were all settled with their sherry and lemonade, Professor Clement started in again. He was seated in a wing chair the twin of Mrs. Clement's, right across from the loveseat where Brenda sat beside Jori. He had been looking at Brenda keenly, the way Jori often did.

"So you believe in mercy-killing, Brenda? You think it's justifiable under certain circumstances?"

Brenda was gripping her glass of lemonade so hard she was afraid it might shatter. The way Mrs. Clement had wafted her into the loveseat had made her feel as if she was taking part in a dance. "Yes," she said, her voice breathy and dry. "I guess I do. If somebody's in a lot of pain, I mean. Or if they have nothing to live for."

"Nothing to live for," Professor Clement echoed slowly. "And how do we decide that another human being has nothing to live for, Brenda?"

"Victor. You're not in the classroom," Jori's mother said, in the same mock-stern tone that Jori had used. Then she smiled at Brenda. *She sees how nervous I am,* Brenda thought. *And she's just trying to be kind.*

"Um, well, we can't decide for somebody else," she answered Professor Clement. "About whether they have anything to live for, I mean." She could feel Jori's eyes on her. There was a tension coming from Jori, like the hum from a tuning fork. She glanced at her. Jori was wide-eyed and nodding a little, giving Brenda an encouraging smile. *Could she be showing me off to her parents?* Brenda wondered, then immediately decided, *No.*

"So each· person would have to decide for themselves. Whether they wanted to go on living or not. And there would have to be laws. To make sure nobody's forcing anybody to do something they don't really want to do. Because everybody's different. I mean, just because I think somebody has nothing to live for, I don't really have the right to . . . ." She stopped, blushing. How could she possibly tell them how easy the essay had been to write? All she had to do was try to imagine herself grown up. Different. Better. Not living with Annie Bray any more. No matter how hard she tried, she couldn't do it. She couldn't see herself as anything other than Brenda Bray, Pleasingly Plump. The only escape would be to get onto Art Bray's bus. And she would. She would hop aboard without a second thought. Any time. Right now.

"You've thought this through, Brenda," Victor Clement was saying. "And you're juggling some weighty ethical issues. Freedom of choice. The sovereignty of the individual. But what happens if that sovereignty is compromised by, oh shall we say, insanity? What happens when the individual becomes a threat to themselves, or to . . ."

"Victor," Mrs. Clement interrupted again, "These girls are in Grade Seven. Not first year university. Remember?"

"I know that, Suzannah. I just happen to believe that . . . ."

"A man's reach should exceed his grasp," Jori interrupted in a playful sing-song. Then her mother chimed in with, "Or what's a heaven for?" And the two of them linked pinky fingers to celebrate saying the same thing.

Professor Clement turned to Brenda and said with an air of mock despair, "You see, Brenda, how a prophet is without honour in his own living room?"

*

"I've told you not to slam that door!"

Brenda has closed the door as quietly and carefully behind her as she ever does. Then, as she tiptoes softly into the house, she hears, "You don't have to stomp! You can walk like a normal human being!"

She ducks into her room and tries to read. Her mother comes after her. "Get up. And put that book down. That's why you're the size you are. Sitting around with a book all day." Brenda heaves herself up again and moves to the living room, then to the kitchen, with her mother following and yapping at her from behind like a little dog. Finally, when she is wedged between the fridge and the table, she turns and faces what she knows is coming.

"Look at you! Just look at you! I think of you walking down the street where everybody can see you and I'm ashamed! Do you hear me? I'm ashamed!"

Brenda hears. And she understands. How could her mother not be ashamed of her? Just look at her mother's narrow, elegant hands, then at her own dimpled paws. How could her slow, lumbering self possibly have come out of quick little Annie Bray?

"I see the other girls coming home from school, and they're so nice and normal and pretty and they have such nice normal pretty friends to walk home with, and I think, Why couldn't I have one of them instead of what I've got? Their mothers are so lucky. They must be so happy. I think about how happy their mothers must be and I cry. Do you hear me? I cry!"

Annie Bray screams until her voice is a whisper, then she whisper-screams some more. About how she had to marry a bus driver because of Brenda and how her own father died because of Brenda and how her own mother will have nothing to do with her because of Brenda. She won't stop until Brenda starts to cry. That's the rule. Brenda knows she could cut things short by letting herself cry as soon as she feels the tears coming. But Other Brenda makes her hold out longer and longer each time.

"And when I think about the day you were born! How I kept telling myself, at least I have a little girl! A little girl! And she'll be so pretty and sweet that her grandmother will just have to love her and everything will be nice and normal again. And what a joke that was! What a dirty, rotten joke! Because look what I ended up with! Look at you! Look at you!"

Brenda lies awake in bed afterwards and imagines Other Brenda standing dry-eyed and scornful before her mother, letting her run out of words. Then delivering cruel, horrible speeches of her own. Speeches like fire that shrivel Annie Bray, make her crumple and moan. What Other Brenda says in these speeches is so huge and terrible that Brenda can't hear the words in her mind. They're like lightning coming down from the sky or lava coming up from a volcano. All she can see is the dark twisting cavern of Other Brenda's mouth. Annie Bray covering her ears, her own lips forming, *No, No, No!*

But it never happens. As soon as she starts to cry, her mother says, "Oh boo hoo, boo hoo. Don't you cry on me, you big baby. I'm the one who should be crying around here." Then she retreats to her darkened bedroom and closes the door.

After that, Brenda wipes the tears from her face and tiptoes into the kitchen and eats half a loaf of bread for supper, holding her breath while she butters slice after slice, listening for sounds of her mother getting up and coming after her again. If she hears her mother snoring, she will add most of a package of processed cheese to the bread, chewing through three slices at once, loving the gluey orange stickiness between her teeth. Then a bowl of cold left-over mashed potatoes, the butter congealed but still delicious. And there is always a gallon or two of Neapolitan ice cream in the freezer. She eats the vanilla, then the strawberry, then finally the chocolate. Her favourite.

She washes the dishes, does her homework and goes to bed at her usual time, telling herself that maybe in the morning the hurricane will be over. Maybe her mother will get up and bathe and dress and make breakfast for her. It will be her way of saying she's sorry, that the good times can start again.

"Have some more," Annie Bray will say, pouring syrup onto another slice of French toast for Brenda. "Go ahead. Treat yourself."

Rae

I wonder what Mrs. Pasquale's daughter is doing these days. I haven't thought about her in years. Mrs. Pasquale must be dead by now – she was a lot older than Annie Bray when they were roommates in the Home.

I never even knew her daughter's name. Dark-haired woman. Thin. Muscled. Fierce bird-of-prey eyes. Stuffing her mother's dirty underwear into a plastic bag. Saying, "If I didn't have to work, she'd be home with me." She spent all of Saturday and all of Sunday with her mother. This after putting in a full work week. Probably had a passel of kids, too. She did everything. Combed her mother's few strands of hair. Fed lunch to her, one spoonful at a time. Swabbed her mouth and hands with a damp face cloth. Helped her into the bathroom, got her onto the toilet, then wiped her afterwards.

Meanwhile, I'd be glancing at my watch every two minutes during the token twenty-five per week I spent in the Home. This after an hour on the GO bus, then half an hour rattling up the Mountain. Then the whole thing in reverse, back to Toronto. Three hours of travel, half an hour of visit. And every week, an almost obscene surge of joy when I heard the Home's door click shut behind me and took the first of seventy-three steps to the bus stop.

I'm in another Starbucks, Jori. This one's at the corner of Wentworth and Queensdale. I actually can't stand these places. But it's a table and a chair and a toilet, and I needed all three. I'd been walking for an hour, zigzagging up and down the side streets the way Brenda used to. Trying to stretch time. Push back the moment when she'd have to confront Annie Bray.

It all came back. That non-stop gnawing in the belly that Brenda tried to soothe with food. Like no fear I've felt since. Not even being questioned by the police after you disappeared could compare to it.

"All right, Brenda. Let's go over it again. You and Marjorie Clement stopped in at Boone's Hobbies, Solly's Variety, Slaine's Notions and Dry Goods and the public library. We have spoken to the proprietors of the stores, and to the librarian, and they do remember seeing you. Then you say that once you were outside the library, you had an argument with Marjorie and parted company. What was that argument about again, Brenda?"

"She wanted us to do something we weren't supposed to do."

"And what was that again?"

I can still feel Annie Bray's skinny little arm tight across my plump shoulders. She snarled up at those policemen like a mother tiger. "My daughter has told you and told you what they argued about! That girl Jori, as she called herself, came up with some hare-brained scheme to go after Clarence Frayne! Clarence Frayne! If she'd listened to my daughter and done the right thing, she'd be safe at home now instead of dead or worse than dead. So why aren't you out looking for that monster instead of browbeating my daughter, who has told you the truth and is so upset these days that she can't even keep her supper down?"

Because they have a feeling your daughter is lying, I thought. *And they're right.* But I said nothing. Just kept my eyes on the living-room rug while Annie Bray tore a strip off two of Hamilton's finest.

The story I was sticking to was that I had never gone anywhere near the escarpment that last day. That you and I had fought about that, and had split up outside the library. Then, while you had headed toward your house, I had gone and sat in the gazebo near where the Jolley Cut meets Concession Street. I had sat there for a long time, I said, because I was too upset about our fight to go home right away.

It had been a tradeoff. Throw Annie Bray and the police a bone of truth. Tell them about your plan to capture Clarence Frayne. Hope it would divert them from the bigger truth about what had happened between you and me that last Saturday at the ledge.

For weeks after you disappeared, I would jump every time the phone rang or there was a knock on the door. I was sure it would be the same two officers. Saying they had found my footprints or something of mine on the path. Wanting to go back over certain parts of my statement. I'd lie awake nights, imagining going to jail for lying to the police. Being visited once a week by Annie Bray, who would scream at me through the bars of my cell about how she could no longer hold her head up in church. For the shame. Did I hear her? *The shame.*

It was Clarence Frayne who let me off the hook. Two weeks after you went missing, police found him camping with some hoboes outside Caledonia. His buddies, who knew him as Bill, said he'd been with them the whole time. But who believes a bum? Especially when the whole world is howling for somebody, anybody, to blame? In the words of the *Hamilton Spectator*, the authorities "failed to persuade" Clarence Frayne to reveal where he'd hidden your body. Maybe because he was telling the truth when he said he'd never seen you. Or because the authorities got a little too persuasive.

I didn't know what to do with Clarence Frayne's death. Execution. Murder. I still don't. Those nights when I wake up at three and can't get back to sleep because every time I close my eyes I see his baby face and bewildered eyes, I remind myself that he did kill five girls. And quite possibly killed you too. But I still can't get back to sleep. Whenever a child is murdered, the public rage that boils up terrifies me. Those people who take a day off work to stand outside a courthouse and scream and throw things? I get scared for the killer. I feel as if it's me being hustled back and forth with my coat pulled up over my head.

When I finally made it to my street today, Jori, I almost walked past my old house. Hardly recognized it. The shutters are red now instead of green. Somebody's built a car port. Planted a Japanese maple in the front yard. It's actually kind of cute. But I swear, that house used to loom when I was a kid. It frowned down at the street. And all because of tiny, terrified Annie Bray rattling around inside.

She was afraid of everything. She would never sit on the side-facing seats of a bus. If there was no front-facing seat available, she would stand. Why? Because a woman had once been thrown from one end of such a seat to the other when the bus came to a sudden halt, and had broken a tooth on the chrome armrest. I never knew if she witnessed this or just heard about it from my father. But every time we got on a bus together, she would hiss in my ear, "Not the side seats. A woman was thrown." It was a mantra. *A woman was thrown.*

If a phone bill came in the mail, she'd pull on boots and go out into a hailstorm if necessary, just to pay it the same day. She might be dead tomorrow, but by God, she'd die with the accounts settled. If she spotted a single dandelion in our backyard, she would put her half-eaten dinner in the oven and go outside with a trowel to dig the poor thing up before it could turn to seed and blow into the neighbours' yards and disgrace her.

Disgrace. Shame. Fates worse than death. Well, she should know. She made one mistake in her whole life, and her own mother disowned her for it.

But not forever. One Sunday morning in church when I was about fourteen or so, I got up out of the pew I shared with Annie Bray, walked across the aisle, sat down beside Thelma Craig and said, "Hello, Granny." It was my little way of saying, *I exist, Bitch, whether you like it or not.*

The upshot was that we turned into something resembling a family. Annie Bray and I started going back to the old lady's apartment for lunch every Sunday. And I actually got a kick out of the old girl. Used to like to tease her about the sermon: "So, Granny, do you actually believe in the virgin birth?"

"I'd just as soon not talk about that kind of thing when I'm having my lunch."

She would have swallowed her tea cosy rather than admit it, but I think she got a kick out of me too. I was a surprise, and not such a bad one after all. She'd had a few bad surprises in her time. Instead of a son to support her in her old age, she'd had a brittle, hysterical daughter who got herself knocked up by a bus driver. Whereupon her husband dropped dead and she ended up in a cramped apartment with nothing to look forward to but weekly sightings in church of the great galumphing blob of a granddaughter who, to her way of thinking, was to blame for the whole fiasco. But then the galumphing blob turned into something Thelma Craig didn't have to be ashamed of. Something with a bit of what she would have called gumption.

80

We came to respect each other, the way old enemies do. "I didn't understand that poem you wrote, Brenda," she would say. (She read everything I wrote, not just the stuff that got published in the high school newspaper. She even gave me a cheque for fifty dollars when I was packing for university.) "I didn't see the point of it." So I would try to explain it to her. She would keep her eyes on her plate the whole time. God forbid she look the slightest bit interested. Then when I was done, she would say, "Well, maybe so. But it seems to me that you don't need that kind of thing."

"Reason not the need, Granny."

I only said it once. But it caught her off guard. She looked up at me, and for just a second before she could mask it, there was a glint of admiration in her eyes.

I'd always wondered what my mother made of my writing career. My success. I used to give her a signed copy of each of my books as they came out. She accepted them with neither thanks nor comment. And I had too much pride – too much of Other Brenda still inside me – to give her the satisfaction of asking what she thought of them.

If she had been the kind of woman to chat to neighbours over the fence, she might have bragged about me behind my back. Worked it into every conversation that her daughter Brenda was actually Rae Brand. You know? The mystery writer? Who writes about old Toronto? But she had no friends, no contacts except for me.

She never once called me Rae. In time, she was the only person left in my life who called me Brenda. And as for my books, save for silently accepting each new one that I gave her, she never acknowledged their existence. Except for once.

It was when I was forty or so. I had just published *The Mount Pleasant Unpleasantness*. I was doing my weekly checkup on my mother. She was still getting by on her own in the house, but she was starting to go downhill. My weekly routine included peeking into the clothes hamper, removing and washing any dirty dishes she had stashed inside it for some reason, then inspecting the fridge to make sure she had something besides a single bunch of wilted broccoli and five quarts of milk, four of them sour. Sometimes I did laundry. Most weeks, I went out and bought groceries for her. It was turning into an all-day marathon, and I was starting to look at brochures advertising something called assisted living.

This particular day, she had greeted me at the door with a funny little smile. An I-know-something-you-don't-know smile. I tried to ignore it, but she followed me around, looking as if she was going to burst. Finally, when I had finished my rounds, I sat down on the living-room couch and said, "All right. What is it, Mother?" (She had been Mother ever since I had become Rae Brand. The more familiar Mom belonged to Brenda.)

She didn't say anything, just picked up a book that had been lying face down on the end table beside her chair. It was *Sunnyside Strangler*. And so help me, it had a bookmark stuck in it. She had been reading me, Jori. And she wanted to talk to me about what I had written. For once we were going to have a real chat.

Or so I thought. No. So Brenda thought. That last little vestige of Brenda, the one I could never quite get rid of, was being suckered in as of old.

My mother opened the book at the bookmark. Got up and came toward me, holding it out with her finger pointing at a spot on the page. I looked. Just below her fingertip was the word "the." Except it was misspelled "hte." She had found it. The one typo Mackenzie and Fraser has ever, in all the years, let slip through. She must have gone through each of my books line by line. Not to read them. Not to enjoy them. Just to find some imperfection. A weak spot.

I looked up from the page into her face. Her smile was a grin now, of triumph. But it was the triumph of insanity.

I got her onto the Home's waiting list as soon as I could. And I finally gave myself permission to hate her. The relief was unbelievable. My first thought on waking was, *I hate my mother.* I'd repeat it to myself throughout the day, like a mantra. And it was kind of like getting religion. Being saved. Jesus loves me. I hate my mother. Same thing.

It actually made things nicer between the two of us. For once, I turned into something resembling a daughter. I arrived earlier for our visits, and stayed longer. Every now and then I would look at my mother, smile tenderly and think, *I hate your guts.* And her unsuspecting little face would open like a flower to the sun.

I thought about her today, while I was looking at that tiny little house I could barely recognize. What was it like for that young widow, left all alone with a baby and some photographs and a medal? What kept her going? What were her joys?

I still have her. A dusting of her, that is. Spencer's Funeral Parlour on Upper Wellington kept trying to sell me an urn, but I stood my ground. Annie Bray would have too, if she'd seen the prices. So she's in a sealed cardboard box that looks like one of those fancy take-out containers that characters in New Yorker cartoons eat out of. I keep her on a shelf in my front hall closet. I don't have a clue what I should do with her. She didn't have a favourite spot where I could dump her. She was such a miserable little cuss, frankly, that I might as well just flush her down the loo.

How on earth did my father get near her? Much less get her *in trouble* as they said in those days? I know so little about their courtship. There was the thing about her sprained ankle. And I remember her telling me once about a traffic tie-up, and the two of them being the only ones on the bus. Sitting talking for ages until the accident or whatever it was up ahead could be cleared. Him smoking cigarettes – you could smoke on buses then – and offering her one. It was her first and only cigarette, and it made her sick. She actually had to stumble out of the bus and throw up.

That's all I have. The story ends there. But maybe that's all it took. Maybe it made a crazy kind of sense to Anne Louise Craig that if Art Bray had seen her vomit, he might as well see everything else. Or maybe she was trying to get away from Thelma and Douglas. Maybe conceiving me was an act of rebellion. Courage, even.

Brenda

"Mrs. Bray, I cannot tell you what an honour it is to meet you at long last. I'm so sorry you were indisposed last week. I trust you are in good health today?"

Annie Bray is standing in the kitchen doorway. Her hands are twisting a tea towel into a rope. There are two dots of colour in her cheeks, as perfectly round as if they were drawn on with rouge.

"Did I see a tea-rose bush in your front yard, Mrs. Bray? How do you keep it blooming this late in the year? My parents have all but despaired of their own tea-roses. Perhaps you could advise them."

The dots are not rouge. They're real. Brenda sees them every Sunday at church when they walk past her grandmother's pew. Annie Bray could almost be ready for church now. She has taken off her apron, pulled up her stockings, combed her hair and put on lipstick. All she needs is a hat and gloves.

"This is a wartime house, is it not, Mrs. Bray? They're so marvellously compact. And they allow for such lovely big yards."

Shut up, shut up, shut up! Brenda wants to hiss at Jori. And at the same time, she wants to hiss, *Say something!* at her mother.

She has worried all week about this visit. Would the drapes be closed when she and Jori arrived at the house? Would Annie Bray have her hair in pin-curls? Would she scream at Brenda in front of Jori about some small thing she had been sitting and brooding about all day?

She started in last night, while Brenda was doing her homework. "Is this going to be a habit? You go to this Jori's place, so she has to come here? Every blessed week?"

"We do our homework together." Not true. Both times, they've just talked and visited with Jori's parents. Brenda has had to get up early the next morning to do her assignments.

"You've never needed anybody to do your homework with before."

"Grade Seven's different. The teachers all say we should have a homework partner."

Another lie. Their geography teacher suggested it once as a possibility. Brenda thought about adding, *it's normal,* then stopped herself just in time.

She has already pushed Annie Bray far enough this week. She imagined Jori using the bathroom during her visit, drying her hands on one of their thin, scratchy towels. The towels in the Clements' bathroom are thick and soft.

"Um, could we start using fabric softener?" She had seen it advertised on TV.

"Why?"

"To fluff the towels up a bit?"

"You don't need that kind of thing."

"But it's only eighty-nine cents."

"What do you mean, *only* eighty-nine cents? What do you know about *only?* Do you know what I have to pay for groceries? *Only* fifteen dollars a week! To feed you! Do you know what those shoes cost that you've already broken down the backs of?

How about your clothes that you're already too big – too fat for? Well? I'm asking. I'm waiting."

Now, in front of Jori, Annie Bray seems to be waiting for somebody to prompt her. She throws a panicked look at Brenda. Brenda thinks back at her all the things she could say: *Welcome to our home. I am so pleased to make your acquaintance. Charmed, I'm sure.*

Mrs. Clement would know what to do. She would offer refreshments. At least ask Jori to sit down. Why can't her own mother act like a normal human being for once? Or better still, why couldn't her father be here instead? Art Bray would kiss Jori's hand. Escort her to a chair. Address her as Miss Clement and make her smile and blush with his talk.

Annie Bray is still staring at Jori, her mouth working a little. Jori is still acting as if everything is perfectly normal. "And these photographs must be of Mr. Bray," she says. "Please accept my condolences on your loss." She is looking at the framed pictures that have hung in the dark hall between the kitchen and the living room for as long as Brenda can remember. There are three of Art Bray in his uniform, smiling his big smile over his double chin, shaking hands with the Transit Commissioner. And there is a fourth, showing Annie Bray shaking the mayor's hand while the Commissioner looks on.

All at once, as if remembering her lines, Brenda's mother starts to speak. "He was named Transit Operator Of The Year." Her voice is dry. "Three years in a row." She points jerkily at the photographs. "That's me accepting his medal for him. He saved a whole bus load of people. The day he died." And then, to Brenda's horror, Annie Bray starts to cry.

Since early morning, Brenda has been trying to imagine all the worst possibilities for how the visit will go, thinking that if she anticipates them, maybe they won't happen. She has imagined

87

her mother wild-eyed and out of control, going on at her in front of Jori about how fat she is. She has imagined her cold and sarcastic, grilling Jori about her high-toned address, her private school, the Anglican church she goes to. The one thing that she has not imagined, and never would have imagined in a million years, is what is actually happening.

"You must be very proud of your husband, Mrs. Bray," Jori is saying, patting Annie Bray's arm and giving her the same penetrating look she gave Brenda that first day at recess. "It must be wonderful to have a hero in the family." Her voice is low, soothing, as if she is calming a frightened animal. "Would you consider showing me the medal? And telling me how Mr. Bray earned it? I don't mean to intrude. And of course I've heard the story from Brenda. But I understand that you were actually there."

Then, while Annie Bray darts into the bedroom to retrieve the little velvet-covered box that has the medal in it, Jori turns to Brenda and says crisply, "I think your mother needs to sit down. And perhaps we could have a sweet drink of some kind? Sugar is good for shock." She turns, marches into the living room and sits on the chesterfield, smoothing the place beside her, waiting for Annie Bray to return.

*

"Marjorie? Dear? I don't think your father can fairly be expected to have known that Mr. Bray had flat feet."

This was two days ago, when Brenda was paying her second visit to Jori's house. Everything looked and sounded the same as the week before. But there was a crackle in the air that reminded Brenda of the moments before a thunderstorm. Did it have something to do with her? Had Jori's parents not liked her when they met her last week, and were they disappointed now to see her back?

Jori stood stiffly, her eyes down, while her father kissed her. Professor Clement sighed as he turned away from her to take Brenda's hand. Maybe they had had a fight at breakfast, Brenda thought. Maybe Jori's father had forbidden her to bring that Bray girl home with her again, and was just waiting until Brenda left to have it out with her.

The second they were sitting down with their sherry and lemonade, Jori glared at her father and said, "Brenda's father died a hero!"

"Oh?" Victor Clement said over his sherry glass. "Really, Brenda? Was it the war?"

"How could it be the war? Brenda's twelve. Just like me. Remember? And how could her father be a soldier? He had flat feet!" That was when Mrs. Clement interrupted to point out that Professor Clement could hardly be expected to know such a thing. And for once she did not correct herself when she forgot and called her daughter Marjorie.

"What say we let our guest tell us the story herself?" Victor Clement said, turning deliberately away from Jori and peering at Brenda from between dropped spectacles and raised eyebrows.

His look made her feel as if she was some rare specimen that he had been searching for all his life. Jori had looked at her the same way at recess that afternoon, while she was pulling the story of Art Bray's death out of her, asking for more and more details. The look embarrassed Brenda. It made her want to warn them that she wasn't really that special, that her story wasn't that interesting, that she was bound to disappoint them.

"Well," she began, "my father was a Transit Operator for the Hamilton Street Railway Company."

"I'm sorry?" Victor Clement interrupted. "A – did you say transit operator?"

"Yes. Um, he drove a bus?"

"Oh, a bus driver! Yes. Of course. I'm sorry, Brenda. I've just never heard it referred to that way before." He glanced over at his wife, who was studying the surface of her sherry and looking as if she was trying not to smile.

Brenda started to blush. Was there something wrong with saying Transit Operator? At home, she had to say it. She wouldn't dare come out with bus driver. But everything here was the opposite of what it was in her house.

Ever since knowing Jori and meeting her parents, Brenda had started to think that her whole life was in bad taste. She didn't know how to act, how to talk, what to wear. There was probably something wrong with the way she was drinking her lemonade right now. And when she started telling the story of how her father died, every word would be wrong, wrong, wrong. The Clements would be ready to burst from trying not to laugh.

But Jori wasn't trying not to laugh. Her eyes were fixed on Brenda, fierce and rapt. So Brenda told the story to her.

*

Now Annie Bray is telling it. And Jori is listening to her as intently as if she had not already heard it twice.

The two of them are sitting side by side on the wine satin brocade chesterfield that used to belong to Annie Bray's father. If Brenda sat on it holding a full glass of ginger ale, Annie Bray would say, *Don't spill on my father's couch* or *Don't break the springs.* But she didn't say anything like that to Jori when she came back out of the bedroom with the medal, her face looking as washed and bright as a pebble after rain.

Brenda is sitting apart from them, on the green vinyl easy chair her parents bought on time from Woolworth's in the first six months of their marriage. The Hamilton Street Railway Company finished paying for it.

"The Transit Commissioner himself told me I'd have nothing to worry about," Annie Bray is telling Jori. "Nothing. And so did the mayor." They are both looking at the medal, nestled in its little box of midnight blue velvet. When Brenda was younger, she used to wonder how something so small could pay for the clothes she kept growing out of, and for all the food she ate. *It's a pension!* she wants to say now, watching the two of them with their heads together. *It's a cheque that comes in the mail once a month. My mother takes it to the supermarket and cashes it. Big deal.*

She has never been so angry in her life. The anger is like a balloon inside her, swelling bigger and bigger, threatening to explode with a bang. She will splatter all over the two of them. All the black, rotten, soupy muck of Other Brenda will coat them, and will soak into her dead grandfather's couch, and she will not care. Just look at them. Jori studying her mother like something under a microscope. And her mother too stupid to know what's happening. Thinking Jori wants to hear all about her stupid life.

How did this happen? How did one thing lead to another, until she was actually opening the door of this house to let Jori Clement come in? She has always guarded this house from outsiders. Kept its secrets. Thanks to her, nobody knows about the mother who goes for days without dressing or bathing. When Brenda comes home and finds the drapes closed, the blank eyeless face of the house is a reminder and a warning: *No one must know.*

Not even the school nurse who summoned Brenda to her office last year and said, "Are you aware that you weigh more than I do?" The nurse was very thin, like a needle. She looked gravely at the silent Brenda, then began to quiz her about what she ate for breakfast. For lunch. For supper.

91

Brenda knew what she had to do without even thinking about it. She had to keep the secrets of the house. All of them. The good things too. The movies she and her mother watch together on TV. The books they talk about over supper. Annie Bray pressing food on her whenever a hurricane has ended. Scalloped potatoes slippery with butter that leaves a shine on her lips. Chocolate pudding sliding in soft, sweet lumps down her throat. And her mother purring in her ear, *Go ahead. Have some more.*

So instead of telling the school nurse about stacks of breakfast toast glued together with peanut butter and honey, she told her about a single boiled egg and a small glass of juice. She turned macaroni and potatoes and pancakes into fish and salad and fruit. She knew the right things to say, from studying the Canada Food Rules in her health textbook. The nurse wrote it all down, looking more and more puzzled.

Now, watching her mother standing up, getting ready to act out the part where Art Bray saves a busload of people, Brenda wonders why she bothered lying to the school nurse. Why she bothers doing anything. *It's not an old movie!* she wants to yell at Annie Bray. *And you're not Katharine Hepburn!*

"Do you know Forest Street, Jori?" her mother is saying. "Right at the bottom of the Jolley Cut? Just past where all the buses turn onto John?"

Jori is nodding, just as if she knows exactly what Annie Bray is talking about. Brenda watches her, thinking, *You've never taken a bus in your life. Your mother has a little red car all to herself, and your father has that big black one he drives to the university. You get driven everywhere all the time – to your gymnastics and your ballet. And now to your acting lessons, too. Because that's what you and your father were fighting about on Tuesday. Not about me. Oh no. Nothing at all to do with Brenda Bray.*

*

"It started at breakfast this morning," Jori told her when she was walking her down to Concession Street after the visit. "I told Daddy I wanted to take acting lessons, and he got all judicial the way he does, and asked me how I was going to fit them in around ballet and school. So I said, well, I guess I could drop ballet. So he started in about all the time I've invested in dance, by which of course he meant all the money he's invested in it. And then he had to bring up ancient history – how I'd dropped gymnastics for ballet, and now I wanted to drop ballet for something else I knew nothing about and might not like and might not be any good at, and how he was starting to see a pattern here, and it was worrying him, and on and on. So I yelled at him that he might think he knows everything but he doesn't because I'm the one who knows what I want and who I am and what I can do. But he doesn't care about any of that and he doesn't care about me and all he wants is a pretty little ballerina for a daughter in a little pink tutu because he's a stuffy old Anglican snob. So then he got all quiet and hurt the way he does and just sat there eating his boiled egg while Mummy started in on me about what a saint my father is and how unfair I was being and how I should apologize. Which needless to say I refused to do. So now I'm *persona non grata* in my own home."

They had reached Concession Street. Jori had stopped talking and was looking at Brenda the way she always did when she finished one of her tirades – as if she expected Brenda to understand exactly how she felt and agree with every word. But this time Brenda didn't understand, and she didn't agree. She never talked back to Annie Bray the way Jori did to her father. She wouldn't dare. And if she had a father like Professor Clement, or any kind of a father at all, she wouldn't call him names while he was eating his egg. She would boil his egg for him.

But she couldn't say any of that to Jori. If she did, Jori might drop her as a girlfriend. And they really must be girlfriends now. Because Brenda has stopped wanting Jori to go away. Instead, she has started being afraid that she might.

Who would she spend recess with if Jori dropped her? Or walk with in line between classes? That had never been a problem before. But it was now. Or it could be. Being girlfriends complicated things.

"Too bad you won't be getting your acting lessons," she finally said, trying to sound as sympathetic as she could.

"What are you talking about? Of course I'll get them. Why wouldn't I get them?"

*

"You know that seat on the bus that's right up front behind the driver's seat, Jori?"

Jori nods and says she does. *Liar*, Brenda wants to hiss at her.

"Well, I knew Art's schedule, so I always used to catch his bus when I wanted to go downtown. And I'd sit right behind him and talk to the back of his head. It was our joke, because there used to be a sign in the buses then that said, DO NOT CONVERSE WITH OPERATOR WHILE COACH IS IN MOTION. So if I started to nag him about anything, he'd point to the sign."

Look at her, Brenda wants to say to her mother. *Pretending to laugh in all the right places. She's laughing at you. Can't you see that?*

But Annie Bray is lost inside the story. It was spring, she is telling Jori. Brenda was a year and a half old. They had caught her father's bus and were heading down to Eaton's to get Brenda a new Easter outfit and Annie Bray a new Easter hat.

Suddenly, without turning his head, Art Bray said, "Annie?"

He didn't sound tense or alarmed, quite conversational in fact. So Annie Bray said, "What?"

"Annie?"

"*What*, Art?"

"Take the wheel."

"Take the *wheel?*" She had never even driven a car, let alone a bus.

"Put the baby down and get up here and take the wheel." He still sounded perfectly calm. But once Annie Bray handed Brenda to another woman passenger and got up to where she could get a look at his face, she saw that it had gone a dark purple. He was clutching his chest with one hand and barely managing the big flat steering wheel with the other.

Annie took the wheel. Together, they steered the bus three-handed down the Jolley Cut, navigating the hairpin turn near the top. Traffic was heavy, and the slope was steep. There was no safe stopping before the bottom.

Brenda started to howl, which got the other babies on the bus going. "It's all right!" her mother yelled at their mothers, who by now were wondering what was going on. "He's got his foot on the brake!"

Art and Annie manoeuvred the bus to the bottom of the slope, then turned onto Forest and brought it to a halt. As soon as it stopped, housewives started to open their doors and come out to see what a city bus was doing on their short little side street. And all the women passengers, with the exception of Annie Bray who was in shock, set up a wail that drowned out their babies. For Art Bray was slumped over the wheel.

"They all knew him." Annie Bray is wiping her eyes again with a Kleenex. Brenda is looking down at her feet, silently mouthing the familiar words along with her mother in spite of

95

herself. "He paid attention to them. He remembered their names. The names of their kids. He'd flirt with the old ladies and pretend to be sweet on the little girls. Women used to send Valentines to the Hamilton Street Railway Company addressed just to Art, or to 'The big guy who drives number 5847.' And every Christmas, they'd get on his bus with little flat boxes of homemade shortbread and fudge for him. There were so many they used to pile up around his feet. And when he used to bring them home, we would . . ."

"That must have made you jealous, Mrs. Bray."

Annie Bray jumps a little, then looks at Jori as if she's just wakened up and found her there. "The same thing happens to my mother. Sometimes my father's female students get a crush on him and phone him at home and practically camp outside his office at the university. And it's all just a cross she has to bear."

Annie Bray is still staring at Jori. Brenda wonders if she should do something. Try to put a stop to what's happening. But part of her just wants to watch.

"In fact, Mrs. Bray, it might be a good idea for you and my mother to get together for coffee. Shall I have her call you?"

Annie Bray picks up the little box containing the medal and snaps the lid shut. The two round dots of colour are back in her cheeks. Brenda holds her breath.

"Or better still, perhaps you could join my mother's women's group. They get together every Wednesday to discuss issues of the day. Right now they're studying the psychology of the modern housewife. My mother says there's a whole groundswell of interest in the topic."

"Oh, I don't know," Annie Bray says, looking down at the box in her hand. "I'm pretty busy. These days." *Doing what*, Brenda thinks meanly, then is sorry. It hurts to imagine Annie Bray at such a gathering. Sitting with one foot hooked painfully around the other ankle. A handful of skirt bunched tight in her fist. A hard, desperate smile frozen on her face.

"But you would have so much to offer, Mrs. Bray! I've heard the story of Mr. Bray's medal three times now, and I can't help thinking that there's a whole other side to it. The part that you yourself played. Because shouldn't you have gotten a medal too? Mr. Bray could hardly have saved that bus full of people without your help. Could he? And that's exactly the kind of thing my mother's group is studying. The way women's contributions have been completely ignored."

Annie Bray gives Brenda a look that says, *What have you brought into this house?*

"So shall I have my mother call you about next Wednesday's meeting? Mrs. Bray? Shall I do that?"

Annie Bray stands up, clutching the velvet box. "It's all right. You girls. You just visit. With each other." She turns and walks toward the bedroom. Brenda can tell from the set of her shoulders and the angle of her head that another hurricane is on its way. It will probably start the second Jori leaves.

The bedroom door closes behind Annie Bray with a soft click. Jori turns to Brenda. "Is everything all right? Did I say something wrong?"

Brenda stares at her. How can anybody so smart be so stupid? Later today, once Jori is gone, she herself is going to have to pay for every word that came out of her stupid mouth. But there's no point trying to explain that to her. "Let's just go to my room," she says, and gets up from the green vinyl chair to lead the way.

*

"I thought the Tooth Fairy was taking them, but it was Mummy, of course."

They were in Jori's room, looking through her keepsake box. She had just opened a little velvet drawstring bag full of her baby teeth. "Mummy kept them all for me. See the little flacks of blood still on them? I can remember when every one of them was pulled. Daddy always did it, with his fingers inside a handkerchief. Mummy kept my baby curls too, see? Look at what a strawberry blonde I was. I didn't start to go auburn until I was three. Red hair runs in my father's side of the family. We're from Iceland originally, and we can trace ourselves right back to Eric the Red. Did you know, Brenda Bray, that someday scientists will be able to take a little bit of your blood or some skin or hair or something, and grow it into an exact replica of you? My godfather is a chemistry professor, and he tells me these things whenever he comes to dinner. But do you realize what that means? It means we could open up graves and bring people back to life! You could meet your own father!"

*

In Brenda's room, Jori walks slowly in a circle, examining each new thing the way she would an artefact in a museum. The walls are pale green, the paint left over from when Annie Bray did the kitchen. Waste not, want not. Three of the walls are hung with Brenda's school diplomas that her mother mounts every year inside black wooden frames she gets from Woolworth's. The fourth wall slants inward, and has Brenda's school projects thumb-tacked to it, each bearing a teacher's red A or A+. Then there is her desk, and beside it her bookshelf, filled with her books. *What Katy Did At School. Little Women. Jane Eyre. David Copperfield.* The oldest ones have Anne Louise Craig penned on the flyleaf in ink-bottle ink.

Jori finishes circling the room. She turns to Brenda, a question in her eyes. "Where are all your diaries?" she asks.

*

"Daddy gives me a new one every year on my birthday. He gives me a pearl, too, for my add-a-pearl necklace, but I like the diaries better. Pearls are so bourgeois, aren't they, Brenda Bray? And they're cruel, too, because it hurts the oyster to have a grain of sand put inside its shell. It's like somebody putting a pebble in your shoe, and every time you shake it out, putting another one in. But I can't tell Daddy that. He makes such a ceremony of it, giving me this pearl every year on my birthday. He even tears up a bit. But at least he gives me the diary. So there they are. Whenever Daddy visits my room, he always goes over to my diary shelf and says, *That's quite a collection you're building there, Miss C.* And I can tell he's just dying to read what I've written. But I know he would never so much as open a single one. He wouldn't even enter this room without my permission. He knows this room is my inner sanctum. Even Mummy has to knock before she comes in. And I must say, that's one thing I appreciate about my parents. They respect my privacy. Because I have to have my privacy. I can't abide the thought of someone else rummaging through my things. That's why I'm so glad to be an only child. Thank God my parents believed in birth control."

*

"How many diaries have you filled so far, Brenda? And where are they?"

For a moment, Brenda doesn't answer. But Jori is waiting, her green eyes sharp as a bird's. Of all the questions she could have asked, why did she have to ask that one? All Brenda can think about is the last time her mother ransacked her room.

"I don't keep a diary," she says finally. Then, hoping to ward off any more discussion, she adds, "I wanted to once, but . . . I just never got around to it."

"You never got around to it?" Jori repeats slowly. "How could you not get around to keeping a diary? That's not something you get around to, Brenda Bray. It's more like breathing or eating or . . ."

"No it's not!" Brenda has had enough. What does this stupid spoiled brat know? With her add-a-pearl necklace and her white satin cushions and her oh-so-clever questions to Annie Bray that Brenda is going to have to take the blame for the second she's gone? What does she know about anything? "A diary's just a book you write in if you haven't got anything better to do." She doesn't really believe what she's saying. But it feels too good to stop. "You don't need that kind of thing."

"You don't *need* that kind of thing?" Jori echoes again in that maddening way. She comes and takes hold of Brenda's upper arms. Brenda can feel her cold fingers denting the fat, and wants to pull away. But Jori's eyes won't let her. "Just tell me this. What would Anne Frank have done without her diary?"

It's a good question. *The Diary of a Young Girl* is sitting right there on her bookshelf. Brenda has read it over and over, imagining herself hiding in an attic and having to tiptoe and whisper all the time, because the slightest noise could mean death.

"Didn't do her much good, did it? She died anyway." Brenda wishes she hadn't said that. But it's too late to take it back.

Jori keeps hold of her arms, her eyes still hard on her face. *This is it*, Brenda thinks. *She'll have nothing more to do with me after this. There'll be no more talks at recess. No more walking home together after school.* She feels a pang, then thinks, *Well, fine. I don't need her. And I won't have to worry any more about her parents liking me, or how my mother's going to act when she comes to visit. Things can go back to normal.*

And they do. That very second. Jori's mouth gets very small and white, her eyes distant. She lets go of Brenda, looks at her watch and says cooly that she must go, and would Brenda please convey her thanks to Mrs. Bray? No, she can see herself out, thank you very much.

The door barely shuts behind her before Annie Bray comes to Brenda's room and starts in. *Who does that girl think she is, asking me questions like that? It isn't normal for a child to talk to an adult that way. And if this is the kind of friend you're going to make, if this is all you can get, maybe it would be better if you went back to not having any friends at . . .*

Jori isn't at school for the next two days. Brenda settles back into her routine of reading her book by herself at recess and walking alone in line between classes. Being without a girlfriend any more is not nearly as bad as she thought it would be. It feels a bit strange not to have Jori's voice constantly in her ear, but she doesn't miss it. Not exactly. Why should she? It would be like missing a dentist drilling into a tooth. Getting closer and closer to the really sensitive spot.

Like that diary business. Why did she have to ask about that?

Brenda did want to keep a diary. She asked her mother for one last year for Christmas. She had seen the one she wanted in Woolworth's – a small thick book with tissue paper pages like a Bible and a little gold lock and key. It was covered in pink plastic, with a pen-and-ink sketch on the cover of an impossibly pretty young girl sitting at a dainty desk and writing with a feathered quill.

The minute she saw the diary, Brenda wanted to be that fantasy girl with her tiny waist and wide-spaced eyes. She wanted her sweetness. The clean, girlish thoughts that must float like butterflies behind her brow. So different from the dark, snarly jumble that the Other Brenda kept filling her own head with.

In Woolworth's she inserted the gold key into the key hole and turned it to the left. *Click.* The diary could be opened. She inserted it again and turned it to the right. *Click.* Now the diary was locked. To all save Brenda. The holder of the key.

She would wear that key on a chain around her neck, she promised herself. And every day, she would reach behind her neck, unfasten the chain, then *click!* open her diary. And every day when she was finished writing, she would *click!* lock the diary again and once more fasten the chain around her neck.

"So that I could write things down," she gabbled to her mother one day while Annie Bray was sprinkling clothes to dampen them for the iron. "So that I could remember things. It's a five year diary, see. And every day I could look back on what I – what we did a year ago or even five years ago." Brenda was sweating, trying so hard to look and sound as innocent as a kid in a situation comedy on TV. Ever since she had started getting her period, her mother had been acting more suspicious of her than usual. Criticizing every little thing. *Don't walk like that. Walk like a lady. Don't swing your purse. Sit with your legs together. That's a dirty-sounding laugh.*

"You could write things down in a scribbler," Annie Bray said reasonably enough now, rolling the sprinkled clothes into damp bundles. "A scribbler costs twenty-five cents. What's so special about this diary you saw, anyway? Is it bound with real leather or something?"

"It has a lock on it," Brenda said eagerly. "With a key. So you can lock it up after you've finished writing in it. And nobody can see what you've been writing."

Her mother stopped rolling up clothes. Turned and looked at her. "What do you mean, *nobody*? Who's the *nobody* who's not supposed to see what you've been writing? And just what kind of thing are you going to write in this diary that you don't want this *nobody* to see?"

It was the start of a three-day hurricane.

Ever since, whenever something Brenda has said or done gets her going, Annie Bray does a shakedown of her room. She crashes Brenda's books to the floor. Yanks her socks and undershirts and nighties like entrails out of her dresser drawers. Shoves the clothes in her closet back and forth on their hangers. All the while grunting, "I'll find it. I'll find it. And I'll read it too!" The diary. The diary in which Brenda writes dirty, hateful things about her own mother. Who has to feed her and clothe her and put up with her all by herself. The diary that does not exist.

On the third day, Jori comes back to school. As soon as Brenda catches sight of her, she wants to run and hide. What if Jori comes up to her and says something? What if she doesn't? Are they enemies now? What do enemies do? How are they supposed to behave?

Then Jori sees Brenda and marches right up to her, beaming at her as if nothing has happened. She hands her a flat, tissue-wrapped package.

"I couldn't stop crying, Brenda Bray. I couldn't eat or sleep, either. Mummy and Daddy both kept coming to my room to reason with me, but I was inconsolable. Then Mummy finally got it out of me what was wrong. She always does. I told her how angry I was with you. And with your mother. I told her every single thing that happened. And do you know what she did? She turned it all around. She told me that I was really angry with myself. Because I'd put your mother on the spot and embarrassed her. And I'd obviously touched a nerve with you too, with that diary business. But open your present! The bell's going to ring any minute!"

Brenda unwraps the package. It is a leather-bound diary, exactly like the ones on the shelf in Jori's room. The year, 1962, is stamped in gold on the spine.

"Daddy got it for you," Jori says while Brenda stares down at the book, wondering what on earth she's going to do with it and where she can possibly hide it from Annie Bray. She looks back up at Jori. It doesn't matter. Nothing matters. Because they're friends again.

"I told Daddy what you said about not needing to keep a diary," Jori says. "And you know what he said, Brenda Bray? He said, *Tell Brenda to reason not the need.*"

Rae

I t's three o'clock. I'm sitting inside a bus shelter near Concession and East Eighteenth. I was on my way to your house, Jori, when I got caught in the rain – a real straight-up-and-down soaker. I'm on my second pen, and I'm two-thirds of the way through this diary.

There goes another bus. They stop and the doors open and the drivers look at me. I wave them on, but they still hesitate. I want to say, What's the matter – never seen somebody writing a book in a bus shelter before?

I guess that's what's happening. But what sort of a book is being written? And who exactly is the author? There. I'm back to wondering whose hand is moving across the page.

You see, Jori, I've always prided myself on never having written a word either as Brenda Bray or about Brenda Bray. I've convinced myself that she plays no part in any of the Elsinor books, that she provides no grist for my mill. No, no, it's *Annie* Bray who has always been the driving force, the engine of my creativity. Or so I've believed. So I've wanted to believe.

What makes my books popular is not their heroine. (Though she does have a fan club – the Elsinor Grey Literary Society. A bunch of dear ladies who dress in period costume and traipse around Toronto with old maps, tracking down the sites of the murders. Poor things usually end up in parking lots and condo courts.)

But for all that, it's never been about Elsinor. Heroines like Elsinor are a dime a dozen. She's the standard loveable oddball, the sweet misfit, the rebellious wallflower who's neither exactly pretty nor downright plain, and has the further handicap of intelligence. The one who's just sufficiently off, in other words, to be kept out of the social mainstream, thus conveniently free to write mysteries and hunt down murderers as a sideline.

What really makes my books work is their villains. And there is nothing generic about them. Every one of my villains is a brown dwarf. Oh, they may disguise themselves as stars, and some of them are very convincing. But Elsinor Grey never fails to see through the phony twinkle to the genuine dullness within.

A brown dwarf is an astronomical wannabe. It's too big to be a planet. And though it's more the size and shape of a star, it doesn't shine. It can't. It might once have been on its way to becoming a star. But something in its makeup was lacking – just the right combination of mass and heat and energy. So it never exploded into stardom. It never shone. Never twinkled. And it never will. It just floats through space, lifeless and dull.

In psychological terms, most of us are neither stars nor brown dwarves. We're more like planets, just doing our orbital rounds. Sure, we'd like to be stars, have our supernova moment. But we resign ourselves to the fact that it's not going to happen. The thing about the brown dwarf, though, is that it cannot resign itself. It hates itself too much for being ugly and cold. But it hates the star more. Its only fire is a burning, seething resentment. Without hope of any real twinkle. No explosion, ever. No beauty.

I'll never forget first finding out about the brown dwarf. It was a Eureka moment. I remember thinking, *My God. That's Annie Bray.*

And so help me, a character sprang fully formed into my imagination. My first villain. Before I had a plot or a sleuth, I had a murderer. I named her Beatrice Love. I gave her Miss Hawkin's sweet face and enormous bust. I made her the kind, motherly housekeeper of one John Melrose, a detective whose lovely young fiancée has just succumbed to a mysterious illness. In his grief, Melrose needs the care and support of dear, kind Beatrice Love more than ever. Which is fine with her, because she's had the hots for him for years. But she knows he'll never look at her and see anything besides a surrogate mom. The only satisfaction she can get is by bumping off her rivals. Starting with the fiancée and continuing with one Elsinor Grey, a writer of mysteries who keeps pestering Melrose with questions about police procedure. And who, having wandered into the kitchen one day for a cup of tea, spots something that doesn't belong among the bunches of dried herbs Beatrice gathers from her garden. Foxglove. Digitalis.

Yes, I knew all about that kind of jealousy-fuelled malevolence. I understood it only too well. Thanks, I assumed then and have gone on assuming, to Annie Bray.

This must be a first, Jori. It could even generate a headline worthy of your scrapbook. MYSTERY WRITER TAKEN IN BY OWN RED HERRING.

Brenda

"What's the worst thing you've ever done?"

It's recess. They're sitting in their usual spot, on the bench outside the utility shed with its scarred wooden walls and rusty padlock. They have fifteen minutes. As usual, Jori has their topic all picked out.

The worst thing. Brenda thinks through her whole life, searching for something that might impress Jori. She always has her homework done. She never breaks a rule or gets into trouble at school. There is the way she touches herself down there at night. But the *Marital Manual* says that's normal.

"Tell you what," Jori says when Brenda has been silent too long. "How about if I go first? Will that help? Okay." She looks at Brenda for a long moment then says all in a rush, "I was kicked out of Glenferris."

"Kicked –"

"*Shhhhh!*" Jori puts her hand over Brenda's mouth. "I'm not supposed to tell anybody." She glances to the left, where a group of beehive girls are standing in a circle and snickering about something. Then she looks the other way, to where two teachers are talking.

Brenda whispers, "You told me your parents took you out of private school because they wanted –"

"I know what I told you. It's what I'm supposed to tell everybody. For the rest of my life. It's even on my record. Miss Hammersdottir – that's the principal – she let me finish my year. Then my parents formally withdrew me from the school."

"Why did they throw you out?"

Jori smiles. "They said I was incorrigible."

Brenda makes a mental note to look the word up later. Though she can guess what it means. "But what did you do?"

"Everything." At Brenda's look, Jori sighs and starts to recite a list. "I talked back. I skipped chapel. I defaced my uniform. That's what they called it, even though all I did was roll the skirt up and loosen the tie, for God's sake. What else? Oh yes. I rewrote the words to the school hymn to make it funny, and passed out copies. I took the *Marital Manual* to school and showed it around. That was the worst thing. But I had to do it, Brenda Bray. Do you know what our old bat of a health teacher was telling us? She was telling us that the pangs of parturition – that's what she called labour pains – the pangs of parturition were God's punishment for Eve's disobedience in the Garden of Eden. She was actually saying that! In the nineteen sixties! So I took the book to school and I showed it to the other girls during Recreation and I said, 'Look. See that hole? See how small it is? Think of a baby's head coming through that. That's why it hurts. Not because of some fairy tale in the Bible.' Well, somebody – and I know who it was, too. It was Hildegarde Buchanan. I'll bet you anything. She always hated my guts. Anyway. Hildegarde or somebody snitched to her parents, and they started phoning the other parents, who started phoning the school. It was all about money. They all threatened to withdraw their precious daughters if the corrupting influence – that's what they called me – was not dealt with. So I had to go. For the rest of the year, they even kept me in a room by myself during Recreation."

"Were your parents mad?"

"Oh God. Mummy's a Glenferris Old Girl. She gave me this cold, polite treatment that she does when she's furious. But that wasn't as bad as Daddy. He cried, Brenda Bray. He actually cried. He took me into his den and asked me to tell him how he had failed as a father, and he was just sobbing the whole time. It was awful. I wanted to kill myself, and I told him so, and that made him cry again." Jori puts her face in her hands and shudders.

Brenda stares at her. She can believe in Mrs. Clement's silent treatment. It would be kind of like a Hurricane Annie, only not as bad. Even the bit about Professor Clement's tears rings true, though she has never seen a man cry. But there is something that isn't making sense.

"Your parents. They're not still mad at you. Are they?"

Jori looks up, surprised. "Oh no. Of course not. Took them a little while, like a couple of days. But they came round. And you know something? It was the school they were really mad at, not me. They think I don't know that, but I do. I heard them talking when they thought I was asleep. Daddy called Miss Hammersdottir Little Hitler. And he said that if any of the faculty ever had an original thought, it would blow their heads off. And he said that the problem was that none of them had the slightest idea how to deal with a child who had been raised to think for herself and form her own opinions and – oh, it was just so great, Brenda Bray! And Mummy was agreeing with everything he said, and I wanted to get out of bed and run to them and hug them both, but I couldn't because I wasn't supposed to be listening. But the very next morning Mummy stopped her cold polite treatment and Daddy called me Miss C. So I cried and said I was sorry and I told them I'd be confirmed after all. Because that was another thing. I was refusing to go to confirmation classes at Glenferris. I said it was religious brainwashing. But then I thought, hell. They're meeting me halfway, so this is the least I can do for them."

She beams at Brenda, who stares back at her. She can't imagine Annie Bray ever forgiving her for being expelled from a private school that cost good money. She doubts she could forgive herself either, or stop feeling the shame. *The shame.* What Jori is talking about sounds like what Reverend Urquhart goes on about every Sunday at Knox Presbyterian.

*

Jesus loves me, this I know . . .

Brenda doesn't have to march downstairs to Sunday school any more. But the words to the children's hymn still make her bunch all her muscles up hard and wish she was deaf.

For the Bible tells me so . . .

She doesn't care what the Bible tells her. She knows better. Jesus might love all the other children, but the best she can hope for is that he'll try to be nice to her. It's not the same as loving but as Annie Bray says, beggars can't be choosers.

Little ones to Him belong
They are weak but He is strong . . .

On the Sunday school wall there is a painting of Jesus surrounded by children. He has his arm around one of them and is just about to put his hand on another one's head. They are all little and weak-looking, just like in the hymn. You couldn't call a single one of them pleasingly plump.

111

Taking children on His knee,
Saying, "Let them come to me."

In Sunday school, Brenda used to look at the painting and worry about what would happen if Jesus suddenly arrived back on earth one day the way he was supposed to. She knew he would let her come to him. But she hoped he would have the sense not to try to take her on his knee. She couldn't stand the thought of him trying to be nice about it. Sweating and smiling and saying, "My goodness. Aren't you a big girl for your age."

Now that she's twelve she doesn't have to go downstairs any more to where Jesus loves her. Instead, she gets to stay upstairs in church with Annie Bray. And with Thelma Craig, who sits just a few feet away but will not turn her face in their direction. And with God, who, according to Reverend Urquhart, loves them all in spite of everything.

God's love, Brenda has gathered from Reverend Urquhart's sermons, is not the same as Jesus' love. If Jesus came back, Brenda would at least be able to see him coming and avoid him by ducking around a corner. But God is invisible and everywhere. No matter where she might hide, God will find her and love her. No matter how bad or sinful or disgusting she might be, inside and out, God will go on loving every inch of her. Including the inches she herself might not love.

Brenda can't stand the thought of anybody loving her that much. Loving her when she's sitting on the toilet. Picking jam from between her toes. It makes her think God might be a bit retarded. She can imagine Knox Presbyterian getting like Annie Bray's pressure cooker from all that demented love building up. She can see the church roof blowing off some Sunday morning, just from God loving each and every one of them so much and for no good reason.

But afterwards, in all the smoking rubble, she knows that there would be one lone figure left standing. Other Brenda.

*

"I'm waiting, Brenda Bray."

Brenda still can't think of anything she's done that's bad enough.

"Okay," Jori says at last. "Let's forget about bad deeds for a minute. What's the very worst thing you've ever wished for?"

Brenda's stomach clenches. This isn't the first time she has wondered if Jori can see right through her to Other Brenda. Other Brenda wishes for all kinds of bad things. Some of them are so bad she can't even imagine her dead father letting Other Brenda onto his bus. "Sorry, Miss Bray. Got room for you, but not for that nasty friend of yours."

Jori is watching her, smiling. "Want me to go first again? All right. This will be like being blood sisters. Only it will go deeper than blood." She pauses, holding Brenda's eyes with her own. "You know how you lie in bed at night and you think about things? How you touch yourself and imagine it's somebody else touching you? Don't look away. Everybody does it. Well, I imagine that it's my father. I want him to be the one, Brenda Bray. I read somewhere that in some societies, that's what happens. A girl's father takes her virginity. Everybody knows it's happening, and it's a big ceremony. And the minute I read about it, I knew it was what I wanted. So sometimes, after we've all gone to bed, I lie in the dark and I send for him. With my mind. I send him messages. *Come to me. I'm ready. Come.* I send them over and over. And sometimes, just when I'm drifting off to sleep, I swear I can see him standing in my bedroom doorway."

113

Her voice has dropped to a whisper. She is still looking hard at Brenda. Waiting.

"I wish . . ." It's all Brenda can say. Jori reaches and puts her hands on her shoulders to steady her. "I wish . . ." What she wishes for is worse than what Jori wished for. It's so bad that until this moment, she didn't even know that she wished for it.

She wishes she had everything Jori has. Her father. Her mother. Her house. Her bed with its canopy and cushions. Her slim body. Her red hair. Her green eyes. Her life. She wishes Jori could go away. Die? Yes. If that's the only way. Stop existing. So that she herself could step into the space where Jori is now.

Jori's hands are still on her shoulders. "Tell me," she whispers. "You can tell me."

She has to say something. But she can't say what she's thinking. "Sometimes I wish my father would come back from the grave. And take me with him." There. It's true enough. And it's probably bad enough to satisfy Jori.

Jori takes her hands from Brenda's shoulders. She sits back and looks at Brenda, as if she wants to say something but can't decide on the words.

The bell rings. Recess is over.

She knows, Brenda thinks as they walk together into line. *She knows that's not the worst thing I've ever wished for. But has she guessed what it really is?*

No. She couldn't have. Because she's still standing beside Brenda in line. And she's smiling at her. Like a friend.

Rae

I 'm sitting in a pew inside Knox Presbyterian. Good old Hard Knox, as I used to call it just to bug my grandmother. The place is still rocking, to judge from the sign out on the lawn. Two services every Sunday. Presided over by one Reverend Jennifer Towers. I'd love to have seen Thelma Craig reacting to a female minister. On some level, she'd probably have enjoyed herself. One more reason to sigh and look pained and keep glancing at her watch.

Why do people still come to these places? To sit on a hard pew in their stiff clothes and have such a terrible time for one hour a week that the rest of their life doesn't seem so bad? I know why I'm here right now. My feet were hurting, and the sign on the lawn said *Open through the week for prayer and meditation*. So I took that to mean, *For taking a load off and scribbling away in the diary your dead friend gave you in 1962.*

It occurs to me that I could wander through the building and seek out Rev. Jennifer and do a bonafide confession. "Bless me, Mother, for I have sinned. It is bloody ages since my last confession, and here is my sin. I didn't exactly kill my best friend – my only friend – when I was twelve. But I destroyed her nonetheless. You don't have to lay a finger on somebody to destroy them." And then what? Forgiveness? Counselling? Maybe she would urge me to go to the police. Confess to lying to them back in 1962. I doubt I'd be charged with anything. I was a twelve-year-old kid with weight issues. Scared to death of a clinically depressed mother. I did consider talking to the boys in blue when that dog found the bone. And it's not fear that's stopping me. I simply cannot see the point of doing such a thing. Even if my revised statement did lend some credence to those remains, so what? What finally happened to you would still be a mystery.

No, I won't waste Rev. Jenny's time. I'm not sure Presbyterians go in for confession. And anyway, I'm not even sure I believe in God. The assumed goodness and love of God, that is. The only god I've ever come across that I think I could endorse is Crow. Also known as The Trickster. Divine goodness and forgiveness do not convince me. But divine sense of humour? Sure. Divine cackling perversity? No problem.

Or maybe I'm missing something. Does Jennifer Towers get up every week and go on about the love of God, the way Timothy Urquhart used to? Do people need to hear that, over and over until they start believing it?

Maybe even Thelma Craig's stony little heart softened a bit on Sundays to the tune of *Jesus Loves Me*. Hard to imagine. She didn't need that kind of thing, remember? When she came to church, she came to church. Literally. She might pay lip service to an invisible God, but what she believed in was Hard Knox. Bricks and mortar she could kick with her foot. And solid oak pews inside, full of people she could pass judgement on.

I've got more of the old girl in me than I like to think, Jori. I am, as Coward put it, no good at love. Divine or human. Giving or getting. Especially getting.

What's a person supposed to do if they honestly cannot stand their inner child? If they measure their happiness in terms of how far *out* of touch with her they've managed to stay? Fuck Brenda Bray. Just fuck her. She had no self-respect. And she got what she deserved. What she wanted, too. She may have been a lamb to the slaughter – more like a fatted calf – but part of her was always watching her own martyrdom and loving it. Thrilling to it. And there was something thrilling about a showdown with Annie Bray. The drama of it. The extremes she could take it to.

Trashing my room, for instance, when she was looking for my diary. That was a show. A performance. And I was – no, not an audience. More like a stagehand watching from the wings. Waiting to clear the set. Put everything back together, so she could do it all over again.

And that's exactly what would happen, once Annie Bray had worn herself out. I would pick up my clothes and tuck them back into my dresser drawers. I would put my books back on the shelves in order, smoothing bent pages, repairing ripped dust jackets with Scotch tape. I would feel sorry for my room. Imagine it frightened and hurt. Needing comfort.

Yeah, yeah, I know. It was Brenda I should have felt sorry for. Should be feeling sorry for now. Well, I'm trying. I've walked in her shoes today. And I have the blisters to prove it.

I went past your house about an hour ago, Jori. Not much about it has changed, except that somebody's painted the front door blue. It doesn't go with the fieldstone. Or with the rock garden. But everything still has that very English look of deliberate carelessness.

You must have landed in the middle of all of that like a bomb. The one bit of craziness in your parents' solid Anglican lives. Their planned child who turned around and ripped up the plan. Well, maybe you were their saving grace. God knows, you were mine.

I visited the gate at the bottom of your street that you used to slip through. It's chained and padlocked now. But all it had in 1962 was a latch. I can see you closing it carefully behind you, then hightailing it down the lane and over the edge of the escarpment, where you'd wait for me. With your mother's kitchen twine and your father's letter opener.

What took you so long, Brenda Bray?

That's a good question, Jori. But I've got a few of my own. Twine? Not rope? Or even duct tape? And your father's letter opener? That's what we were going to threaten Clarence Frayne with? I held the thing in my hands more than once. It wouldn't cut butter.

Have you seen this little girl?

Had anybody? Ever?

Your mother overdosed on her tranquilizers, vomited while unconscious and ended up in a coma. "That's what happens," I remember Annie Bray saying with an odd note of satisfaction in her voice. "You try to kill yourself with pills, but it backfires and you end up worse than dead."

She may have inadvertently saved my life, saying that. I was home from the hospital and had stopped trying to starve myself to death. But every now and then, idly, almost playfully, I would toy with alternative ways and means. *Walk outside one night in your pyjamas and freeze to death maybe?* Too late. Spring's coming. *Sneak the bottle of aspirin out of the medicine cabinet and swallow it down?* Oops. Might end up like Mrs. Clement.

Then one day in the school library I came across a poem:

> *Razors pain you;*
> *Rivers are damp;*

118

Acids stain you;
And drugs cause cramp.
Guns aren't lawful;
Nooses give;
Gas smells awful;
You might as well live.

I remember thinking, Jori could have written this. I wanted so much to read it to you. I started to cry, and kept on until they had to send me home from school. But at least I had a credo: *You might as well live.*

When I was in university, Annie Bray sent me a clipping about your mother *finally succumbing.* "That means they pulled the plug," she said in her letter. "Probably her husband told them to. He's head of classics at McMaster now."

Your parents hit the news largely because of you, Jori. You were forever "missing since 1962, believed to be the final victim of mass murderer Clarence Frayne." Even your father's obit, which took up half a column in the *Star* a few years ago, gave you that particular nod.

Time to move on. The ledge awaits.

Brenda

"**B**renda. Listen to me. There's been talk. People have been talking. All along Concession Street. Mrs. Slaine especially. Mrs. Slaine knows you. She's seen you in church every week since you were a baby. And she's been going on about this red-haired girl who doesn't go to Knox, so she doesn't know her name, but she can tell that she has you wrapped around her little finger."

"We don't do anything to Mrs. Slaine. We just look at stuff in her store. On our way to the library. To do our homework."

"Mrs. Slaine's not a fool, Brenda. Not when it comes to running a store, anyway. She thinks Jori's there to shoplift. And she thinks she's using you – your good name and your good reputation – as a cover."

"She's not there to shoplift. And she's not using me."

"Then what's she doing with you?"

It's Saturday morning. Brenda knew something was up when she smelled pancakes and link sausage – her favourite breakfast – and came into the kitchen to find Annie Bray fully dressed and out of her pin-curls. It's not her birthday. Or the aftermath of a hurricane. She eats cautiously while her mother talks, slicing her sausages into dime-sized discs.

"Brenda, I've never told you this. But you're old enough now. When your father died, I thought it was the end of the world. I was all alone with a baby, and I was still practically a baby myself. And through the years the only thing that's kept me going was the thought that maybe your father's watching me. Rooting for me somewhere. Saying, *It's okay, Annie-girl. You're doing fine.*"

Brenda looks up from her plate. Does her mother imagine Art Bray coming for her in his bus, the way she does? Her mind pushes the thought away. The bus is for her and her father. Nobody else. Even though Annie Bray is wiping her eyes now with Kleenex, and Brenda herself can hardly swallow.

"The thing is, I know I haven't done just fine. As a mother. I know things aren't always right. Normal. The way they should be. Between us."

"It's okay."

"No it's not. I wonder sometimes why you don't hate me, Brenda. You should. You have every right to. Sometimes."

"I don't. You've been fine." A tear rolls down the side of Brenda's nose and lands on her plate. She sops it up with a piece of pancake and eats it.

"And you might not believe this, Brenda, but I've tried to like Jori Clement. For your sake. I've told myself, There must be something about this girl. Something worthwhile. Because if there wasn't, my daughter who is so smart and so fine wouldn't have anything to do with her. So I've tried to be decent to her, Brenda. Even though I know she laughs at me behind my back."

"No she doesn't."

What Jori does behind Annie Bray's back is try to analyze her. Two weeks ago she decided she'd rather be a psychiatrist than an actress, and she's been using Brenda's mother as her first case study. *Have you noticed how she practically runs out of the room whenever I'm at your house, Brenda? Obviously, I represent some kind of a threat to her. And it's always the bedroom she retreats to. Interesting. Interesting.*

"Oh, it's all right," Annie Bray is saying. "She can laugh at me. Maybe the two of you have a big old laugh together."

"We do not!"

"I know that's all part of growing up. And you'll be a teenager soon. Imagine." She gives Brenda a tremulous smile. "You'll be in high school. Going to parties. Dances. Starting to go out with boys."

Brenda looks down at her chubby fist curled round her fork. She can feel her double chin buckling against her neck. What is her mother talking about?

"And that's another thing. When I was a girl, I . . . I made a mistake, Brenda. A big one. The biggest mistake a girl can make. I was just lucky that your father was a good, decent guy at heart. He could have been the other kind. He could have walked out on me and skipped town. Lots do. Because I was just smitten. I was head over heels. If that man had asked me to jump off a cliff with him, I'd have done it. So I know what it's like to be taken with somebody. To think that they're the only person on earth. I know how that feels, Brenda. And I can see it happening to you. And it breaks my heart. To think what this Jori Clement could do to you. Once she's gotten tired of you. Or figured out that you're not going to do whatever she wants you to. She's going to drop you like a rock, Brenda. She's going to throw you away like trash. And you're not trash! You're my daughter! And you're the finest, best person I know."

*

"You have an air about you, Brenda. I'm sure you've been told this before. But I look at you and I see strength. Stability. Maturity. Everything my daughter needs to help her through this difficult period."

Victor Clement was slumped in his wing chair, watching Brenda while she scrubbed the carpet on her hands and knees. Jori had just run screaming out of the living room, followed by Mrs. Clement.

It had all started as usual. Just before Mrs. Clement called to them both to come for lemonade because Professor Clement was home, Jori was showing Brenda the latest additions to her scrapbook. There were no new headlines like GIRL GIVES BIRTH TO FISH or DEAD MAN RIDES NEW YORK SUBWAY FOR TEN HOURS. Instead, there were pages and pages of articles about the escaped child-killer that everybody was starting to talk about.

"Clarence Frayne," Jori murmured to Brenda, slowly leafing through the scrapbook. The same pair of bewildered eyes looked up at them from photograph after photograph. "Isn't that a beautiful name?"

"Yeah. I guess. But . . ."

"But what?"

"Well, think of what he's done."

"What about what he's done?"

"He killed five girls. He strangled them. How can you just put that out of your mind?"

"Who says I'm putting it out of my mind?"

Jori had been talking in riddles like this ever since the story about Clarence Frayne escaping from the Kingston Penitentiary hit the newspapers. She gave the impression of enjoying some huge secret, and sometimes looked as if she was listening to music nobody else could hear. It all made Brenda want to pop her like a balloon.

"How can you collect pictures of a killer? And how can you think he's beautiful? And that he has a beautiful name?"

"Because he is beautiful. And he does have a beautiful name."

"But he's crazy!"

That almost popped it. Jori gave Brenda the same look she gave her when she said nobody needed to keep a diary. Brenda was just about to take back what she had said when Mrs. Clement called to them to come into the living room for their lemonade.

*

"I've tried to think what your father would say about Jori Clement, if he could be here, Brenda. And I have a feeling he'd say, *Annie-girl, our daughter's growing up. You have to let her go. You have to let her spread her wings and make her own mistakes.*"

Annie Bray blows her nose. Brenda can hardly taste her last mouthful of pancake and sausage. The kitchen clock is a blur. Is she going to be late for her meeting with Jori? Does it matter? Is she even going to go? Jori's plan is crazy. They'll never find Clarence Frayne. Much less capture him. And even if they did, what would they do with him? Sneak him into Jori's room and hide him under the bed?

Here in the kitchen, listening to her mother, Brenda can see how ridiculous it all is. Stupid. Like two little Grade Ones digging down to China, or building a rocket ship out of cardboard boxes and trying to fly it to the moon. But when she meets Jori under the edge of the escarpment, all that changes. Something in Jori's eyes, in her whispery voice and quick, alert movements, makes Brenda start to think, yes, maybe it might work. Clarence Frayne has to be somewhere. Why not there? Somebody has to find him. Why not the two of them?

"So I'm going to leave it up to you," her mother is saying while she picks up plates and puts them in the sink. "Maybe when you see Jori today you'll find the strength to stand up to her and put a stop to what's been going on between the two of you."

Something in Annie Bray's voice makes Brenda look up sharply, then down again at the space where her plate just was. She feels her face getting warm. Does her mother know about the other thing she and Jori have started doing? Does it show? Maybe her mother can see it in her eyes when she comes home from their Saturday excursions. She has no words for what they do, only a dark, delicious feeling that wells up in her when she thinks about it. She tries not to think about it. It's wrong. It's not normal. They've got to stop. Soon. Last time, she pushed Jori away and whispered, "What if somebody comes along the path and sees us?"

Jori gave her a long, tender smile. She said, "He would understand."

"You just go along, then," Annie Bray is saying now, starting to run water into the sink to do the dishes. "Do whatever you're going to do. But know that I trust you to do the right thing. And that your father would too."

*

"My daughter has always been an emotionally delicate child, but lately . . ." Victor Clement sighed. "Oh, I know she's at the age to develop crushes. She's got a bit of a one on me at the moment, though you wouldn't guess it from this afternoon. But this Clarence Frayne obsession. I don't know. There's no point trying to forbid it. You saw what just happened."

He was silent for a moment. Brenda scrubbed the carpet, first with the wet cloth, then with the dry. It wasn't her own spilled lemonade, but it felt right for her to scrub it up.

"You see, Brenda, Suzannah and I have always treated our child more like a friend or a colleague. We've answered all her questions. There's never been any of this *wait till you're older* business. We've encouraged her to make up her own mind and defend her own opinions. And you just saw where that can lead. But the alternative doesn't bear thinking about. We had to take her out of Glenferris. We simply had to. Trying to wrestle all that imagination and individuality into a uniform every morning was tantamount to torture. Not that they wanted to let her go. Oh no. She was one of their top students. But Suzannah and I thought that the public school system, with its more secular focus, its more cosmopolitan makeup – oh, we thought a lot of things."

He was silent again. Brenda crouched motionless near his feet, staring at the damp patch on the carpet. She had looked up the word incorrigible right after Jori told her about being kicked out of Glenferris. It meant bad beyond reform. She could imagine Jori coming across it in a book or something, then looking it up and thinking, Yes. *That's what I'll be. Incorrigible. Bad beyond reform.* Except, the story she had told about her father crying when she was kicked out had seemed so true. As true as the story he himself was telling now. So which of them was lying? Jori or her father? She started scrubbing again.

"Anyway, Brenda, at times like this I worry that Suzannah and I may have turned our child into something of a social freak. She does not fit in. She does not make friends. Never has. That's why we were both so delighted to hear about you. And the minute I saw you, I thought, *Oh thank God.*"

Brenda wished she could scrub the carpet forever. She kept one ear cocked for sounds of Jori and her mother coming back. This was the end of the friendship. It had to be. It had almost ended once before over the diary business. But this was worse. Jori would never forgive her for witnessing what had just happened.

*

Brenda is cutting across Inch Park on her way to meet Jori outside Boone's Hobbies. Hurrying so as not to be late. She was so close to deciding not to go. But then her mother practically pushed her out the door.

It's a cold, bright morning. Jori's favourite kind of day. There was a frost last week, and it changed the last of the green leaves to yellow and orange almost overnight. "Welcome to my season," Jori has said more than once, looking out over the city while she waits for Brenda to cross the ledge. "Isn't it glorious? Can't you just hear the trees celebrating? They've finally gotten rid of that stupid green that made them all look the same. And isn't it brilliant that Clarence Frayne would choose this season to go free? Isn't it perfect?"

How many Saturdays has it been now, Brenda wonders, crossing Queensdale Avenue on her way to Concession Street. Clarence Frayne escaped in the last week of September. And now it's almost the end of October. Next week is Halloween. Only five Saturdays, then, including this one. How can that be? It feels as if she and Jori have been doing this forever. Even though she can remember exactly when it all started, and why.

*

If only Jori hadn't brought her scrapbook with her into the living room. Professor Clement noticed it under her arm while he was kissing her, and sighed. He put his hands on her shoulders, looked seriously into her eyes and said, "Sweetheart? Princess? Daddy has had a very trying day. And I don't think that Clarence Frayne is a very pleasant topic of conversation just now. Especially when we have a guest."

"Brenda is every bit as interested in him as I am."

Brenda looked down at her saddle shoes. She knew Jori was counting on her not to call her bluff. It gave her a small thrill, even though she knew it was wrong.

"Be that as it may, young ladies," Professor Clement said, giving Brenda a surprised look. "I'm sure we can all find something in this wide universe besides a homicidal maniac to talk about."

Jori flounced onto her end of the loveseat and started deliberately leafing through her scrapbook, snapping each page as she turned it. Brenda sat carefully down on the other end. There was that same crackle in the air she had noticed two weeks ago when Jori was mad at her father about the acting lessons.

Mrs. Clement handed Brenda her lemonade and said, "I understand you girls are studying the art of debate at school these days."

Brenda nodded, turning the glass in her hands and trying to ignore Jori. "We had to say what our personal opinions were? About each topic? And then our teacher made us take the opposite side."

"Excellent!" Professor Clement said a bit too heartily. "That's the point of debate, isn't it? A rational, unemotional examination of an issue, from all possible sides."

Jori snapped a page so loudly that they all looked at her, then looked away.

"So what's your topic, Brenda?"

"Capital punishment. Jori and I are on the same team, and we both said we were opposed to it, so now we have to defend it."

"I wish I could be a fly on the classroom wall when you do!" Professor Clement said, slapping his knee. "Don't you, Suzannah?"

Jori raised her head from her scrapbook and looked at her father. "Why?" she asked dangerously.

*

Brenda is just a few steps away from Concession Street when she stops and stands still. As soon as she rounds the corner, Jori will be able to see her from outside Boone's Hobbies. But what if she doesn't take those few steps? What if she turns around right now and goes home? Or goes directly to the library by a different route and really does do her homework for a change?

She sighs. It wouldn't work. Jori would just pester her on Monday morning at school. *Where were you, Brenda Bray? Were you sick? Why didn't you phone me?*

She is going to have to put a stop to this. Her mother's right, even though she doesn't know the half of it. There are just too many secrets to keep. There's the diary hidden on the top shelf of her locker at school. She hasn't written anything in it, but she still doesn't dare take it home where her mother would find it the next time she did a shakedown of her room. Then there are all the lies she's told about what she and Jori do on Saturday mornings. It would be so easy for Annie Bray to check with Miss Hawkins and find out that they hardly spend any time in the library at all. And once she knew that, she would go on and on at Brenda until all the truth came out. Maybe even the truth about what she and Jori do once they're past the ledge. When Brenda tries to think about what they do, it's like trying to think about a dream after you're awake. She doesn't quite believe in it, even though she knows it happens.

She is still standing on the sidewalk, watching the cars going back and forth on Concession Street. Just a few steps more, and Jori will be able to see her.

It's the same as standing frozen at the ledge. Part of her wanting to go forward, the rest of her wanting to stay put. Once she's crossed the ledge, she's in a whole different world. Jori's world. The path turns a corner, then dips down. The sounds of traffic fade. The sounds of wind and birds get clearer. The two of them start pretending to look for crevices in the limestone that could lead to caves.

"He could be just an arm's length away from us right now," Jori reminds her. "He could be watching us. Listening to us. He could be as close as I am to you now." Then everything turns into Jori's voice in her ear. "He could be you," she breathes. "You could be him. Be him. Please. Be him." Then the whispery little kisses, all around her ear and down her neck until that sweet swelling happens between her legs and she almost moans.

It's too much. Too many secrets. She can't keep them all. She's bound to let one of them out, and then another will follow, and another.

Brenda takes the few steps to Concession Street, and turns the corner. In the distance, she can see the sun glinting on Jori's red hair. The sight makes her feel tired. How long has Jori been standing there waiting?

The ledge. She'll do it at the ledge. She'll say the words. Put a stop to it. All of it.

*

"Well, Mar – Jori, since you ask, I suppose the reason I'd like to be present to hear you and Brenda debate an issue like capital punishment is that I'm an educator. And I have an interest in the development of young minds."

"If you have an interest in the development of young minds, how come we can only ever talk about what you want to talk about?"

"Well, I don't think that's quite the case."

"It happened five minutes ago! You censored this conversation! You forbade Brenda and me to discuss Clarence Frayne!" She was pounding her fist on the scrapbook.

"Marjorie. You are not being fair to your father. And you are embarrassing our guest. Give me the scrapbook, please. Right now." Mrs. Clement's voice was calm. But her lips were pale and her eyes hard. Jori, to Brenda's surprise, got up and did what she was told. Then she sat back down and snatched up her lemonade. Her knuckles were white gripping the glass. The ice cubes clinked.

"Do you think you'll find it very difficult to defend capital punishment, Brenda?" Mrs. Clement was smiling again, just as if there had been no unpleasantness. "Do you have strong views on the subject?"

Brenda's mouth was dry. She tried to ignore the sound of Jori's quivering breath right beside her. "Well," she said, "it's just that, if somebody does commit murder, isn't that a sign that they're insane? And they couldn't help it? So maybe instead of punishing them, we should try to cure them?"

"Well, that's the compassionate view, Brenda," Victor Clement said. "And when it comes to genuine insanity or crimes of passion, I'm right with you. But what about, oh say, a paid assassin? Someone who deliberately and cold-bloodedly plans the murder of another human being. For profit. Don't you think the state is justified in taking an equally deliberate and cold-blooded approach in dealing with – oh, Sweetheart!" He was looking at Jori. "No. Don't do that."

Jori was crying silently into her lemonade. Her face was mottled white and red, and her lips were stretched back over her teeth. Mrs. Clement got up out of her chair and came toward her daughter. She didn't say, *Stop that crying, you big baby,* or, *I'm the one who should be crying around here,* or any of the other things Annie Bray would have said. Her face reminded Brenda of paintings she had seen of the Madonna. She tried to embrace Jori, but the girl knocked her arms away. Her glass of lemonade tumbled to the carpet, where the liquid pooled at her feet like urine.

"Compassionate!" she screamed at her father. "What do you know about being compassionate? That's just a word to you! Just another sound you make with that big mouth of yours! You don't care. You don't care about Clarence Frayne. And you don't care about me!" Then she got up and ran from the room. Mrs. Clement threw a helpless look at her husband and hurried after her.

"Oh. My. God," Professor Clement groaned. He sounded as if he was saying, *Here. We go. Again.* He got up out of his chair and walked out of the room without looking at Brenda. She heard him rummaging in the kitchen. When he came back he had a wet dishcloth in one hand and a dry tea towel in the other. He held them out as if not sure what to do with them. Brenda got up, took both cloths from him and knelt beside the wet patch on the rug. She righted Jori's empty glass and started to scrub at the stain, first with the wet, then with the dry.

Victor Clement settled back into his chair with another groan. Brenda could see his tan wingtip shoes out of the corner of her eye.

"Brenda, I am so very sorry," he began. "I can't tell you how often this kind of thing happens. That doesn't excuse it, of course, but I do want you to know that you yourself are in no way involved. Or responsible."

Brenda scrubbed harder.

*

"What took you so long, Brenda Bray?"

Brenda shrugs. Looks away. Now that she's decided she's never going to do this again, the thought of going through it all one last time makes her almost sick.

"We'll have to skip Boone's and Solly's," Jori is saying, giving her a piercing look, "and go straight to Slaine's."

"I don't want to go into Slaine's."

"Why not?"

"Mrs. Slaine's been talking to people. About us."

"Good! That's the point, isn't it? It's a sign the plan is working."

Plan. "Look, Jori. I'm not feeling so good this morning. How about we just go straight to the path and . . ." She almost says, *and get this over with.*

Jori looks at her for a long moment. Maybe she's going to tell me to go home to my mother, Brenda thinks. Since I'm being such a big fat baby. Except Jori would never say anything like that.

"We have to at least go into the library. All right? Just the library. And don't worry. I'll handle Miss Hawkins. Like I always do." Jori turns and walks quickly along Concession.

Look at her, Brenda thinks. *Not even looking back. So sure I'll follow her.* And she does.

*

"You see, Brenda, there's only so much that parents can do. For the simple reason that they are parents. Suzannah has been the Rock of Gibraltar this last couple of years. But she has her limits too. She's actually on medication right now for her nerves.

133

That calm of hers is deceptive, believe me. And I'm no good at times like this. I should have known better than to step all over my daughter's ego just now. Her pride. I should have remembered that she's at an age when I'm bound to be her hero. And whenever I do demonstrate that I have feet of clay, it's devastating for her. For me, too. I see myself through my child's eyes, and it's not a pretty sight. Then I start to imagine her seeing me at other times. I went into her room the other day. She was out with her mother. I don't know why I'm telling you this, Brenda, but I know you'll have the wisdom and maturity to keep it to yourself. I went into my own daughter's room and looked in her diaries. Oh, I can rationalize what I did, as a parent. I was concerned. Worried. I suppose I could even pull the old *This is my house, therefore everything in it is mine* business. But the fact is, I was just plain curious. Well, I got my comeuppance, let me tell you. I opened diary after diary, and I could hardly believe . . ."

He stopped suddenly and sat up straight, listening. Brenda stopped scrubbing and listened too. Had they heard something? Were Jori and her mother returning? No.

Professor Clement slumped back in his chair. "The diaries were blank, Brenda. Not a word. Not a single word written into any of them. I kept pulling them off the shelf. Turning the pages. It was frightening. It was almost as if my daughter didn't exist."

Brenda was scrubbing the same spot over and over. Thinking about the single diary hidden in her locker at school. How she would love to open it and write in it with a special pen she would buy with her allowance saved up. A fountain pen. How she would love to fill page after page with her best handwriting in real ink.

"Well, my daughter does exist. No doubt about that. And her mother, God love her, helped me put that diary business in perspective. I had thought I was giving the child a gift every year. Giving her my blessing to express herself. But I was actually doing the opposite. I was imposing my will. Or at least, that's how it must have seemed to her. And the tipoff, Brenda, was her asking me to pick up a diary for you. You are the key to the whole thing."

Brenda scrubbed. She didn't want to be the key.

"So I'm going to impose upon you one more time. I'm going to ask you to be Marjorie's – well, not her keeper or anything like that. Her companion. Her confidant. Her diary, in effect. Can I ask that of you, Brenda? She needs someone her own age to listen to her and, oh, go where she's going. I know I probably shouldn't be burdening you with all this. And good lord, you shouldn't be doing that! What am I thinking of? Here. Give me those."

He stood up. Brenda saw the wingtips coming closer, then a hand reaching down. She gave him the cloths and the glass. He turned and took them back into the kitchen. Alone, she got up off her knees, wondering what to do. She couldn't just sit back down in the loveseat, as if nothing had happened. Maybe she should sneak out the door and go home.

All at once, like something in a play, everybody came back into the living room. Professor Clement entered from the kitchen and stood by his chair. Mrs. Clement guided Jori through the other door, one hand on her shoulder.

Jori was pale, and her eyes were downcast. As if on a cue from her mother, she walked woodenly toward her father, arms outstretched. He gathered her in a bear hug and said a muffled "That's my girl!" into her hair. They stayed wrapped around each other for so long that Brenda had to look away. When Victor Clement finally released her, Jori walked stiffly toward Brenda and stood in front of her, not meeting her eyes.

"I'm sorry, Brenda," she said through barely moving lips. "You are my guest, and I should not have subjected you to such

135

disgraceful behaviour. Please accept my apology." She sounded as if she was reciting something she had memorized. Her eyes met Brenda's for just a second. They were narrow and hard.

"Brenda, we all apologize, and we would all like very much for you to come back again next week and give us a chance to redeem ourselves," Mrs. Clement was saying. "But just now I think it would be best if you let Marjorie see you out. Marjorie?"

Jori looked at Brenda again, then turned toward the door. She followed her outside. They didn't speak until they reached the sidewalk.

"You know what this means, don't you?" Jori said tightly.

Brenda nodded. She knew. She was never to talk to Jori again at school, or walk with her between classes, or let on in any way that there had ever been anything between them.

"All right. We'll start this Saturday. We need some way to cover our tracks. But don't worry about that. I'll think of something."

Start what? Think of what?

Jori must have seen the look on Brenda's face, because she said, "Leave the methodology to me. Just come along and be with me, Brenda Bray. Okay? I need you to be with me on this." She drew a deep breath and her voice broke on her next words. "Because nobody else is."

"Jori. Be with you on what?"

For just a second, Jori looked as if she might start screaming at Brenda the way she had at her father. Then she relaxed and looked tenderly into Brenda's eyes. "Just think about him," she said softly. "All alone out there. He ran away because they were going to kill him, Brenda. And if they find him before we do, they'll shoot him down like a dog."

Brenda opened her mouth, but before she could say anything Jori placed her fingertips over her lips. "Don't think about what

136

he's done," she said. "That's all anybody ever thinks about. Don't be like them. The whole world is like them. Just try to think about how he feels. Right now. It gets dark so early these days. And cold. Has he had anything to eat? Is his mouth dry? Is he shivering? Are his hands chapped and raw? Are his feet blistered and bleeding?"

"But how could we . . ."

"Shshsh." She put her hands on Brenda's shoulders. "He's hurting all over. Just think of that. Even if we get to him this Saturday, he'll be hurting all over, all week long."

She leaned slowly toward Brenda and kissed her softly on the mouth. Brenda was so surprised that her mouth stayed a little open. She had never had such a kiss before. It was dry, but lingering. She could feel Jori's breath on her upper lip. And something stabbed her, deliciously.

Jori leaned back, her hands still on Brenda's shoulders. "Until tomorrow," she said, smiling into Brenda's eyes.

All the way home, Brenda kept raising a hand to wipe her mouth. But then at the last minute she would put her hand down again.

*

Now Brenda scrubs her hand back and forth across her mouth until her lips feel raw. But it's not a kiss she's trying to erase. Not this time.

The words aren't on her lips any more. They're not even out in the air where she could chase them and grab them and stuff them back into her mouth. They're inside Jori. She could tell the exact second they went in. She could see it in Jori's eyes.

Brenda is sitting in the gazebo that has perched on the mountain brow for as long as she can remember. Anybody can come here and sit, but nobody ever does because pigeons have splattered the benches. She can hear the pigeons in the eaves, burbling to each other like old ladies in church. *Did you hear? That Bray girl. Did you hear? That Jori.*

She keeps watching to see when Jori comes back up from the path. She knows Jori won't see her. Even if she glances in the direction Brenda would have gone, she won't look into the gazebo, because nobody's ever there. But Brenda will be able to see her. She'll see the sun on her bright hair as she heads through the gate, and she'll know she's all right.

It's been an hour.

Maybe Jori's waiting for her to come back to the ledge and apologize. Standing sulking on the path where Brenda last saw her.

It's been more than an hour.

Maybe Jori found a path down to the access road and hiked home a different way, to make her worry. To make it look like her threat has come true. *Walk that ledge, Brenda Bray. Or you'll never see me again.* Except she couldn't know that Brenda would wait and watch for her. And anyway, they would have to see each other again on Monday at school.

Two hours.

Or maybe Jori continued along the path without her, farther than the two of them ever went. Really looking for Clarence Frayne. Seriously examining the cliff walls for fissures that could be the mouths of caves. Maybe she found one. Maybe Clarence Frayne was in it. Maybe she's stroking his back right now and murmuring to him. Maybe he's already put her down for a nap.

More than two hours. Almost three.

Jori's home. That's it. She's been home all this time, sitting on her father's lap and sobbing about how mean Brenda was to her.

Brenda scrubs her lips again. It had felt so good at the time, like finally bringing up what was making her sick. Is that how Annie Bray feels when she screams and screams during one of her hurricanes? But what about afterwards?

*

"Oh, come on, Brenda. You know you can do it. You've done it before."

Maybe if she hadn't kept Jori waiting and made them late. Maybe if there hadn't been that touch of impatience for once in Jori's voice. Or if she had said *Brenda Bray* instead of plain *Brenda*.

"No," Brenda said. "I'm not going any farther." Then she took a deep breath and added, "Because I'm not going to do this any more."

Jori looked at her for a long moment. When she spoke, her voice was tender. "Don't be scared."

"I'm not scared."

Jori braced herself against the cliff wall with one hand and reached the other out to Brenda. "Here," she said smiling. "Just take my hand, shut your eyes and we'll do it on a count of three."

Brenda could imagine Professor Clement saying that when he pulled out one of her baby teeth. "I said I wasn't scared."

Jori pulled her hand back. Stopped smiling. "All right," she said, "if you're not scared, then what's the problem?" Now she reminded Brenda of Mrs. Clement.

After a long moment, Brenda answered. "I don't want to do it any more."

"Do what?"

"You know."

"Why not?"

"It's disgusting. It's abnormal."

"No it's not."

"It's wrong."

"No it's not."

"Yes it is! You don't know everything!"

Jori flinched back, almost losing her footing. The fear in her eyes egged Brenda on. "You don't know anything at all! You're just a spoiled stupid brat who gets every single thing she asks for and who thinks the whole world revolves around her! Because she's her daddy's little princess!"

It was Other Brenda, finally opening her mouth. She knew she should stop her, but it felt too good to stop.

"I've got news for you. You're not your daddy's little princess any more. He's given up on you. He told me so while I was cleaning up the mess you made that time you spilled your lemonade. And you get on your mother's nerves so much she's taking drugs. He told me that too. You're not even incorrigible. Your parents took you out of Glenferris because you were such a freak. You were embarrassing them. Just like you embarrass me with your highfalutin talk at school and your stupid ideas. And your lies. All that garbage about keeping a diary, when you can't even keep one yourself. Because that's another thing your father told me. He went into your room. Your *inner sanctum*. And he looked inside every one of your diaries. And that's the only reason I'm even here. That's the only reason I've pretended to go along with your stupid plan. Because your father asked me to. He asked me to keep an eye on you. To be your keeper. And you're crazy enough to need one!"

Jori was very pale. Her lips had almost disappeared, they were so white, but Brenda could still see them shaking. She raised both her hands, palms toward Brenda, pushing at the air between them as if trying to push Brenda's words away.

"Please," she whispered. "Just walk the ledge. Okay? Just walk the ledge one more time and then we can – then we'll see."

"No."

"Just one more time. Please?"

"Why should I?"

"Because . . ." Jori was attempting a wobbly smile, trying not to cry. "Because if you don't walk that ledge, Brenda Bray, you'll never see me again."

Brenda looked at her for a long time. Then she said, "Good." And turned. And walked away. She kept listening behind her for Jori to say something. Get the last word in, as usual. But no word came.

*

Three and a half hours.

The light is changing. There are long shadows across the floor of the gazebo. The pigeons have stopped gossiping overhead.

Annie Bray has probably phoned Mrs. Clement by now. Found out that Jori came home hours ago. Phoned the police. Or worse, set out to search the neighbourhood herself. Brenda can see her, racing up and down streets, kerchief knotted under her chin, eyes huge. If she finds her here in the gazebo, she'll start a hurricane right on the spot. Better start for home and try to head her off.

A bus rattles by on Concession Street while Brenda stands waiting for the light to change. *Need a lift, Miss Bray?*

No. That was just a daydream. Even when she was a little kid, she didn't really believe her father would ever come for her. And she knows for sure that he never will now.

Rae

I've asked myself what might have happened if I'd crossed the ledge one more time, Jori, the way you begged me to. Would the presence of a second girl have discouraged whoever or whatever you met up with around the corner? Maybe. Maybe not.

I'm in the gazebo. Yes, it's still here. Hasn't changed a bit, either. The pigeons could be the same ones that murmured about you and me all those years ago. I retraced the steps I took that last day we were together. Walked the path as far as the ledge, then just stood there. I thought about crossing it. Following the path on the other side to where the bone was found. But there would have been no point. It's not about the ledge. It never was.

I stood there and remembered how you looked the last time I saw you. The hurt in your eyes. I remembered what I said to you. And I thought through what I should have said. What Brenda should have said:

Jori, it's all too much. Your complicated, crazy mind. Your weird talk. Your add-a-pearl necklace and your scrapbook from hell. Your diaries that might be full or might be blank. Your private school that might or might not have thrown you out. Your drugged-up mother with her old world manners and your classical scholar father who might or might not be molesting you in the night. It's too much for me. I don't know what to do with it all. I want to be normal. I want to be that pretty, vacant-eyed girl on the pink plastic cover of the diary in Woolworth's. But I don't have a chance as long as you're with me. Looking at me the way you do. Right through the fat. Right down deep inside me to where Other Brenda lives. Other Brenda, who you recognize. And who you love.

There. That's what it was all about. What it's still all about. You loved me. You were this mysterious, fucked-up, magnificent creature who for some reason sought me out and befriended me and loved me. Me. Brenda Bray.

I couldn't let that happen. I had to put a stop to it. You were just about ready to explode, Jori. God knows what you would have become. But you'd have shone. You'd have shone so bright.

And there I would have been. Too dull to reflect your glory. Terrified that the day would come when you would look at me and see me for the brown dwarf I was.

I should have trusted you, Jori. I should have had a little faith. In both of us.

I'm on the last page of your diary. I know now why I was never able to get past *Dear Jori* all those years ago. It was because I wasn't ready to write the last two words. But I am now. So here goes. Are you proud of me?

Love, Brenda.

About the Author

K.D. Miller's first collection of short stories, *A Litany in Time of Plague*, was published in 1994. Her second collection, *Give Me Your Answer*, published in 1999, was short-listed for the inaugural Upper Canada Brewing Company's Writer's Craft Award. *Holy Writ*, a series of personal essays which explore the link between creativity and spirituality, was published in 2001. K.D. Miller is a founding member of Red Claw Press (www.redclawpress.com). She lives in Toronto. (www.dawnwriter.com)

ELAINE BATCHER